MAGGIE,

I Love You

MAGGIE, *I Love You*

RONALD R. HIGGINS

Kravitz & Sons

INNOVATORS IN PUBLISHING, MARKETING AND ADVERTISING

Kravitz and Sons LLC
204 E Arlington Blvd. Suite B
Greenville, NC 27858

Published by Kravitz and Sons LLC.
ISBN: 979-8-89639-406-8(sc)
ISBN: 979-8-89639-405-1 (e)

Library of Congress Control Number: 2025917278

This book is dedicated to all those people that wanted to write and publish a book.

CHAPTER ONE

It was another hot, muggy day in the city. I was sitting at one of those outside cafes in the village. New York is excellent for tourists, but it's even better for the locals. It was hard to believe two years ago I was working for a big Insurance Company as an Assistant Vice President. Brent Stewart is my name. I hated the job, but it was the only thing I could do at that moment. I wanted to go into Private Detective work, but I didn't have the money at the time now here I am today independently wealthy.

When I won that million-dollar lottery, I had no idea I was going to parlay it into ten times that much in the stock market.

The company I worked for was one of those well-known Insurance Firms that shall remain nameless. There was a lot of politics as there is in most companies today. I got tired of it and hated to come to work each morning, so when I won the lottery and invested it in the stock market, and it paid off. Well, I took my shot.

After that, it was easy to go to school and get my P.I. License and open my office: all this and a female chauffeur named Maxine.

Then one day last week, I walked into my office as I did every morning around nine AM. Vera, my secretary, handed me my mail and morning coffee and greeted me with a smile I have come to love. Vera is one in a million secretary. She always greets me with a smile that translates to "Well, Brent, are you ready for another exciting day?"

For the life of me, I can't figure out why some man hasn't married her yet. She is a beautiful woman. She could easily pose for a Fashion Magazine or marry any man she wanted but hasn't so far. She always seems to anticipate what I am going to say or do before I do it. At first, it annoyed me. After a while, I got used to it, and now I enjoy it.

While going through my mail that morning, Vera buzzed me and said I had a call on line two. I didn't know when I answered it; it would be a voice from the past.

I said, "Hello. Who is this?"

The voice said, "Brent, Brent Stewart, is it you?"

"Yes. Who's this?" I said.

The voice came back, "Alex!"

Five years ago, and I still remember Alex Lomax. Nam 1975. We were both Military Police stationed in Saigon. After we both returned to the states in 1976, I lost track of him.

"Alex, how are you doing?"

"Not so good, that's why I'm calling you."

He went on, "I hear you're a big P.I. The man now with your own company. What's it been 1976 since I last saw you? It doesn't seem like it's been four years."

Before I could say anything, he came back with, "I need your help, I'm in trouble."

I knew right then it must be something terrible for him to say that. I've known him for six years, and he never sounded that desperate. In Nam, he was always the one to come to my rescue. He forever had things under control, even when he wanted to marry that girl from Saigon and bring her back to the states. The Company Commander was giving him all kinds of flak, but he always remained calm and stood his ground.

Her name was Maggie Chong. She was beautiful; she spoke perfect English. She said she learned it from the missionaries when she was just a girl in Saigon. Her parents sent her to a missionary school to learn English.

She worked at the Headquarters building on the base. Alex met her, or maybe I should say ran into her. He knocked her down while running into the building. It was love at first sight for both.

"What's wrong?" I said.

"Maggie has disappeared."

"How long has she been missing?"

"A week, I don't have any idea where she went. She's never done anything like this before."

He sounded distraught, so I said to him, "Calm down and let me have your address. I will be there in thirty minutes or so, stay where you are until I get there."

The address he gave me was on Motts Street that was in the heart of Chinatown. I told Vera where I was going.

She said, "I know. I called for your car; Maxine should be downstairs when you get there."

Now there's a woman for you, Maxine. She came to me shortly after I opened the business. She was looking for a job as a mechanic. I never saw a mechanic that looked like she did. She was about five feet eleven and had long blonde hair. She looked like she could have come off a swimsuit calendar. She knew cars, and she wanted a job working on mine. I had two Rolls and one Mercedes Convertible. They are all in top condition, thanks to Maxine. I found something else out about Maxine that comes in handy in this business; her favorite hobby is martial arts. If you think about it, I got a two for one package. That explains her far-east philosophy about everything.

She hasn't had to use it yet, but if the time is right, it's nice to know I can count on her. She's high up in the art. She acts as my chauffeur and bodyguard. Not bad for a kid from Brooklyn.

I smiled at Vera and just said, "I'll see you later."

When we got to the address, I told Maxine, "Wait for me."

The building was an Oriental bar and restaurant with apartments upstairs. The name of the bar was the 'Choy Inn.' I went inside. It had the typical Oriental motif. You know a sculpture of Buddha and flowers and pictures of Chinese Buildings all over the place. You could smell the incense all around. There were about four tables occupied. I thought Chinese food must be in this year.

A beautiful Oriental hostess came up to me and asked with the slightest hint of an accent, "Can I help you?"

"Yes. I'm looking for Alex Lomax."

"Alex and Maggie, they live upstairs. Please, go through there and up the stairs."

She pointed to the door just to my left.

I said, "Thank you."

The paint was peeling off the walls in the hall, and the railing was a little shaky.

Except for that, it looked in pretty good shape. I got to the door, marked one, and knocked. The door opened, and there stood Alex. Although I wasn't sure at first, he changed somewhat. Alex always had a way of looking younger than his years. Only this time, he didn't. Alex was heftier than I remembered and looked like he had been drunk for about a month, which also surprised me. When we were in the Army together, he never took a drink.

He said, "Hi." Opening the door as he spoke. It was a lovely homey apartment. There was an end table next to the couch with a lamp and a picture on it. It was a picture of him, Maggie, and me in Saigon. I remember when it was taken. You could see how happy he was then. As I looked around the room, I could see even after just a week it was missing the woman's touch. Clothes are draped on the kitchen chairs, and empty beer cans were still on the kitchen table and the coffee table. I sat down on the couch. He brought me a can of beer, and I asked him to tell me what he knew about Maggie's disappearance.

"About a week ago she received a letter from her father, he lives in San Francisco, asking her to come to him right away. She got an airline ticket for San Francisco leaving that night before she could use it, she disappeared, leaving the ticket behind."

I had to ask the next question.

"Alex, is it possible she was seeing somebody on the sly?"

He was very calm when he answered, which made me believe he was sure of himself.

He said, "Maggie and I are still very much in love with each other."

"Did you report it to the police?"

"Yes."

"Tell me, did Maggie have a job?"

"Yes. Maggie is the only one who has been working for the past six months. I got laid off for about six months. I worked as a driver for a meat-packing place down by the docks."

"What kind of work does Maggie do?" I asked.

"Well, she works as a private secretary for a law firm on Park Ave."

"Do you have the letter she received from her father?"

He said, "Yes."

Then he removed the letter from the drawer. I asked if he had any other messages that Maggie had received from her father within the last year. He took another one out of the drawer. This one had a postmarked nine-months earlier.

"Is it alright if I hold on to these for a while?"

"Sure, go ahead, if it'll help."

"Well, I don't know how much help they will be, but I have a friend downtown that might be able to tell me something from the handwriting."

Well, I had everything I needed to get started. "Is there anything else you could tell me about Maggie that I don't already know?"

"Well, she had been acting funny the last month as though something was wrong. I asked her if there was anything wrong, she said no. But it was the way she said it that made me think something was wrong, but I didn't press it."

"Well, you stay put while I do some checking around. Do you need any money?"

He said, "No. Maggie and I have a joint account with some money we had put away when we both were working."

I said okay and left. On my way, uptown, I started thinking about how situations have a means of turning around. When we were in the Army together stationed in Nam, he was my Sergeant. I was just a Corporal. I used to follow him everywhere to learn things from him. Now things are turned around, and he needs to find items out from me. Something bothered me about the job he had. When we were in the service together in Nam, all he talked about was that when he got out, he was going to go into Law Enforcement. He wanted to get his gold shield. So, what happened, why didn't he? He didn't look in too good a shape to answer that question. I figured I'd wait and ask him another time.

When I got back to the office, I told Vera we had another case and told her Alex's' story. I also told her this one was a freebie.

She put one of those knowing grins on her face and said, "I assumed as much."

"Would you get me a cup of coffee while I look at the two letters Alex had given me?"

As she handed me the coffee, I said, "Would you call Bill down at the station, and ask him what he knew about a missing report on Maggie Lomax?"

"I already did that, and Bill said he would fax you a copy of the report."

I should have known better. I just smiled and said, "Thanks, Vera, your one in a million."

I didn't notice any apparent difference in the two letters as I examined them. Of course, I was no expert either. I decided to go down to the station and get that missing report myself. While I was down there, I could find out about these two letters. When I was getting up to leave, Vera came in.

"Your car is downstairs, and Maxine is waiting. I called Bill and told him you were on your way."

Vera has been my secretary from the beginning, and she never ceases to amaze me.

"Vera, sometimes I get a distinct impression your eavesdropping on my mind."

She just smiled and said, "I just know my boss." Then she gave me one of those winks I've grown to love.

I walked out, shaking my head, and smiling.

When I got down to the station house, it was busy for this time of day. Bill Singer's office was upstairs. When I walked into the station house, an old Sergeant was sitting at the front desk. He was a gray-haired gentleman that had about twenty-five years on the force and was waiting for retirement. They called him Pops. He was helping some young policemen book a woman that looked like she had been giving personal services to the male population of the city.

He looked up and saw me. As I headed for the stairs, he waved and said, "Hi Brent. What's new?"

I just smiled and said, "Nothing, Pops. I'm just going to see Bill Singer."

"He's in with the Captain."

"Thanks."

Bill Singer and I go back a few years I was still working for the Insurance Company. Bill was a patrolman then. He was going to give me a ticket for illegal parking. I had just come out of a restaurant with a date named Kathleen Connors. I tried to talk him out of it, but there was no changing his mind. I saw him eyeing Kathleen the whole time. I called him off to the side and made a deal with him.

I told him if he didn't write me up, I would set him up with Kathleen. He said okay, so I introduced the two of them, and now she's his wife. We've been friends ever since. Go Figure. When I got upstairs, Bill was leaving the Captain's office.

"Bill, how's it going?"

"Brent. What can I do for you?"

"I'd like to see that missing report on Maggie Lomax."

"Sure thing, The report is in my office. Come on it"

One thing about Bill Singer, he was as neat as a pin. I have never seen anything in his office out of place. I'm sure the character from the odd couple is based on him. I went in and sat down on his couch, and he handed me the report. I read it. There wasn't anything in the statement that Alex hadn't already told me.

"I have a couple of letters Alex gave me. Can you have your boys in the lab check the handwriting and see if it's all from the same person?"

"Sure. I'll send the report to your office."

As I got up to leave, I asked him how long-ago Alex contacted him about Maggie.

"She had been gone seventy-two hours when he had decided to call it in."

"Thanks, Bill."

As I left, I told Bill to give Kathleen a big kiss for me; I turned and headed out the door.

Bill smiled and said, "Brent, are you in love with my wife?"

I turned back at him, raised my arms, and said, "She's one in a million, one in a million." I smiled and walked out.

I decided to stop in at Joes' on the way back and see if Sammy knew anything through the street vine. As Maxine pulled up in front of Joes' and stopped, I told her to wait. I got out and went inside. Every time I go into this place, I feel overdressed.

Joes' was a sports bar. They had one of those six-foot televisions, and the only thing I ever saw on it was sports.

Mostly cabbies and bus drivers frequented the place. I have been coming here since I got out of the service. Janie and I grew up together in Brooklyn; she owned the bar.

I went and joined the Army and didn't see her again until I got out. Janie is one of those people that has a great personality. She's great with people and knows how to get them to like her. Janie was a people person. She was never what you would call pretty. Although, you could always depend on her to give you a shoulder to cry on whenever you needed one. Janie was sitting at her usual spot behind the bar.

"Janie, old girl, how the hell are you?"

"Brent, what brings you to this neck of the woods?"

"Sammy, around?"

"Yeah, he's talking to Lily, the cab driver."

Sammy is the head of the grapevine in this part of the city. If anything is coming down, Sammy knows about it, he has a newsstand on the corner a few blocks from here, and he knows all the gossip.

I walked over to Sammy and Lily. He saw me coming and jumped up and started to run. I grabbed him by the shirt.

"Take it easy, Sammy."

"Brent, I didn't do anything. Honestly, I didn't."

"Easy, Sammy. I never said you did. I have a couple of questions for you. Okay?"

"Yeah, sure, Brent. What is it"?

"Have you heard anything about a woman getting kidnapped in Chinatown? Say in the last two weeks or so?"

"Last two weeks, heh?" He thought for a minute and then said, "Words out the Rizzio brothers are looking for someone that picked up payroll from their cocaine deal. That's it."

"Okay, Sammy, if anything comes up, you know where to reach me."

"No problem, Brent, I'll look out for you."

A week had gone by, and I still hadn't heard anything from Sammy. Come to think of it; nobody had seen Sammy in a couple of days now, according to Janie. Vera buzzed me on the intercom.

"What's up, Vera?"

"Bill Singer is on the line."

"Okay, put him through. Hello, Bill? What's up?"

"Do you know a guy by the name of Sam Wilson?"

"Yeah, that's Sammy, he has a newsstand in the village."

"Not anymore. We just found Sammy floating in the East River."

"I'll be right down. Where are you?"

"East fifty-ninth near the bridge."

"I'm on my way."

I headed over to the pier, where they found Sammy. I couldn't help thinking about what he said about that cocaine deal.

Did Sammy find out who picked up the money from that deal, and that's why he is in the river?

Well, it was a cinch; he wasn't going to do much talking about it. He also wouldn't be able to tell me if he found out anything about Maggie being missing.

When I pulled up in front of the pier, they were driving away with Sammy's body. Bill was finishing up. He walked over to me.

"Sorry, Brent. Did you know Sammy very long?"

"Yes, he was one of my contacts. I've known him for about five years. Did you find anything that could help?"

"Just this."

He handed me a pair of broken chopsticks. I asked him where he found them.

"They were in his coat pocket when we fished him out of the river."

I looked at them. The chopsticks had writing on each stick that said, Koon Lees. I wasn't familiar with the place.

"Well, at least you have someplace to start."

"Yeah, right. I'll let you know what we find out."

Bill started walking away. He stopped and turned around.

"Oh, we also found this picture on him. Anybody, you know?"

As I looked at the picture, I felt a headache coming on. It was a picture of Maggie. I didn't want to tell Bill until I had time to check it out myself.

"She's pretty, but I don't know her. You know how these Asians' are; they all look alike."

"Right, Brent. Well, I'll keep in touch."

All I could think about was to get to Alex before the police. I told Maxine to take me back to Chinatown. I had to see Alex.

When I got, there Alex wasn't in. I asked the Hostess in the restaurant if she had seen Alex. She said she hadn't seen him for a while. I went back to the office to see if there were any messages from him. I hoped he didn't start playing detective. I told Maxine to wait downstairs. I went up; Vera was sitting at the desk as usual. "You have a visitor," Vera said. I went inside. Alex was sitting there looking shook up. I gave him a drink and asked him what was wrong.

"I heard from Maggie; she's okay. I don't know where she is, and I'm worried. There was a knock on my door, and when I opened it, this note was tacked to the door."

He handed me the note. It read, "Honey, I'm fine, don't worry about me. I'll be gone for a couple of weeks."

"Well, that takes care of that."

"No, Brent, you don't understand, as long as we've been married, she never called me Honey. We made a deal not to call each other pet names like that."

"So, what are you trying to say?"

"I'm not sure; I just think something is wrong."

"You mean you think she was trying to tell you she wasn't all right without letting whoever was with her know?"

"Yeah, that's what I think."

"Is there another entrance to your floor beside the restaurant entrance?"

"No. Whoever it was, they would have had to come through there."

"Look, the police found an old friend of mine floating face down in the East River this morning; he had a picture of Maggie in his coat pocket. Do you have any idea how he could have gotten it?"

"No, I don't...wait a minute. A couple of weeks ago, somebody broke into our apartment through the bedroom window while we were out eating dinner. Nothing was gone when we got back except a few pictures of me when I was in the service in Saigon. There was also one picture of Maggie gone. Maybe that's the one you're talking about. There was no money stolen. We thought the whole thing was a bit strange. Then again, we knew this was a strange city and crossed it off to that."

"Okay. Come with me. I'm taking you back to your apartment. I have a few questions for the Hostess in that restaurant. What's her name?"

"Suzy."

"That figures."

When we got there, I saw Suzy sitting at the bar. I sent Alex upstairs and told him to stay put in case Maggie called. Then I walked over to Suzy. She had this beautiful skin-tight dress on with the Oriental collar. It was red and black.

"Hi, Suzy."

She turned and looked at me. If I didn't know any better, I'd say she was glad to see me. Those almond-shaped eyes she had, made me feel like I was back in the Far East again. She had a beautiful smile.

"Hi, what can I do you for you?"

"My name is Brent. You remember me; I was here earlier to see Alex."

"Yes, I remember."

"Well, I'd like to know if you saw anyone come down the stairs by Alex's apartment after I left last week?"

"Yes, as a matter of fact, I did."

"Do you know what he looked like?"

"Yes, except it wasn't a man, it was a Woman."

"SHE! What did she look like?"

"I'd say she was in her middle forties, short, gray hair. Oh yes, she had one of those hats; you know the kind cabbies wear."

That description sounded just like the lady that was sitting with Sammy when I spoke to him last week.

"Thanks. You've been a lot of help."

"Anytime. Why don't you come back to see me later when you are not busy? I get off at eight tonight."

She smiled a smile that was hard to ignore.

"You may have something there. Later then."

I decided to go back to Joe's and have a little talk with Lily, the cabbie. First, I asked Maxine to drop me off at the garage. I figured I'd pick up the old Rx7 and give Maxine the rest of the day off. No use, asking for trouble with a female chauffeur in that part of the Village. Besides, I didn't know how long I'd be or where I'd be going next.

As I drove to Joe's, I kept asking what Lily the cabbie had to do with all this. Also, why was a picture of Maggie found in Sammy's pocket?

When I arrived at Joe's, Lily wasn't there, so I decided to talk to Janie.

"How's it going, Janie?"

"Fine, Brent. You know this is a pleasant surprise. Do you realize this is the second time in as many weeks you've been here? If you don't watch out, it might become a habit."

"What can I say, Janie, when you're right, you're right. Say I want you to know I'm sorry about Sammy. Did he have anybody to take care of the funeral expenses?"

"Yeah, well, he had no family that I know of except us, Brent, so we buried him."

I gave Janie a couple a thousand and told her it was to help with everything. I asked her about Lily.

"Haven't seen Lily since they found the body; she never even showed up at the funeral."

"How long did she know Sammy?"

"The two of them have been hanging' round here together now for about eight months. I don't know how long they've known each other."

"Do you have her address?"

"No, but Mousey over there knows where she lives. He lives right next door to her."

Janie pointed out Mousey to me in the corner. As I went over there to him, I knew the name fit. He was a little guy about five-foot-two or so, very thin, and almost bald on top. As I approached him, I could see a scared look on his face.

"Hi, Mousey, mind if I join you for a few minutes? I have a few questions for you."

"No, no, of course not. Say, could you buy me a beer?"

I turned to Janie and signaled for two beers; she said okay.

"Mousey, do you know where Lily is?"

"Lily? No, the last time I saw her was the day before they found Sammy. She was talking to some guy outside."

"What did he look like."

"You know the type, three-piece suit, and pointed shoes. It looked like the man was wearing a piece. He was giving Lily an envelope. She opened it and took out some money and counted it, and then put it in her purse."

"What happened next?"

"Nothing, he just turned and walked away."

"Can you take me to where she lives?"

"Sure, she lives right next to me in the same building. She's not home. I have been watching and listening for her."

"Well, let's go look anyway."

Mousey lived in one of those old apartments in South Brooklyn on Second Street just below Third Avenue. He had apartment five, and Lily had number Seven. I thanked Mousey and told him to wait inside his place, and I would be back. I didn't want him to see me open her apartment. I wanted to check it out, and the fewer the witnesses, the better. I took out my trusty old credit card and slipped it in the door. It opened as if I had used a key. I walked in, and something or somebody hit me on the head. I went down hard.

When I came to, it was dark. I found the light switch and turned it on. When I looked around, the place looked like a tornado had hit it. Just then, Mousey walked in.

"Mr. Stewart, are you okay?"

"Yeah, except I need a new head. How long have I been out?"

"Only about half an hour, I heard someone run down the hall, and when I opened the door, someone took a pop shot at me. My door now has a hole in it; it didn't have before."

"Did you get a look at him?"

"No, it was too dark."

"Okay, look, here's a ten spot. Don't say anything about this to anybody understand? Nobody."

"Sure thing, Mr. Stewart."

"C' mon, I'll take you back to Joe's."

"No, that's okay. I'm in for the night."

I looked at my watch it was seven o'clock. I headed over to see Suzy. I needed a change of pace. It's not often I get hit on the head. My mother used to say when you lead with your head into a dark room. It shows that you're not using it for what it was intended. I'll have to tell her she was right again, the next time I see her. My head was killing me. Maybe Suzy could help me forget it for a while anyway. I'll bet she could. It was almost eight o'clock when I arrived at the restaurant. I stopped at the office and changed clothes, took a quick shower.

I decided that since I had a few minutes, I would stop up and say hi to Alex and see how he was doing. I knocked on Alex's door. After a minute, he answered. He looked like he had been sleeping.

"Hey, Brent, you find out anything?"

"Yea, that my head shouldn't be the first thing to walk into a dark room. How are you doing?"

"Doing okay, I guess.

"Yea, well hang in there, and something will turn up, I'm sure."

"Brent, you always were a positive person; that's one of the things I liked about you."

"Yeah, well, now I'm going to spend some time with the beautiful girl that works right below you."

"So, she was telling me, only she wasn't sure you were going to show up. I told her you would. Be careful; she is a nice kid."

"You don't have to worry about that. You know me well enough to know I wouldn't do anything to hurt Suzy."

"Yes, but I've seen you hurt yourself before. Remember a little girl in Saigon named Wendy?"

"Yeah, well, I see what you mean. Don't worry, old buddy."

I didn't mention what happened at Lily's apartment because I didn't want to worry him. When I went inside the restaurant, Suzy was standing at her usual place at the end of the bar. As I approached her, she got this big smile on her face. I could tell immediately she was glad to see me. The Asians were noted for their lack of outward expression.

"I'll bet you didn't think I would be here."

"Your right, but your friend Alex knew you would."

"Are you ready, Suzy?"

"Yes, let's go."

When we got outside, it had started to rain. I asked Suzy where she would like to go.

"Don't laugh, but I'm starving, could we go to eat?"

I laughed as I said, "Sure, where would you like to go?"

"I don't know you pick a place."

I knew this beautiful quiet place up on the East Side. Appropriately it was called, 'A quiet little table in the corner.'

It was on the bottom floor of the Executive Hotel on east 38th street. When we arrived, we were having one of those summer rains. The streetlights were reflecting off the wet pavement. The air had that fresh smell like everything was being cleaned. It brought back a lot of memories of growing up in the city that I grew to love. They can have their Cape Cod up north and Monterey on the West Coast. I'll take good old New York City.

I got lucky and found a parking place about a half a block from the restaurant. The rain slowed down enough for us to get inside before we got too wet. We ran to the door, and I looked over at Suzy, and she was laughing while we ran. When I got to the door, I grabbed the door handle and almost fell on my ass. Suzy started to laugh again.

"Great, I almost fall and bust my ass to open the door, and you start laughing."

"I'm sorry; you just look so funny."

She put her hands on my face and kissed me.

"C' mon, let's eat."

I watched her as she walked inside, and I knew I liked this kid. The waiter found us a table for two. There were beads strung down the entrance to the booth like a curtain. We could see out, but no one could see us. There was light with a string on the outside of the cubicle. The waiter told us to pull it if we wanted some service.

After the waiter had left, I looked across at Suzy, as usual, she had this beautiful smile. Her hair was just wet enough, so the ends stuck to her neck and shoulders. She looked like something out of a dream.

"What are you thinking, Brent?"

"Uh...nothing. I was admiring your beautiful face."

"C' mon Brent be serious. What are you going to order?"

Come to think of it; I was saying some trite things. I guess it was the rain. Then again, maybe it wasn't.

"I don't know," I said as I looked at the menu.

"I'll order the New York cut medium-well. What about you?"

"Well, the boneless breast of Chicken sounds good with string beans. What do you think?"

"Sounds good. What would you like to drink?"

"A Margarita."

Just then, the waiter came to take our order. I told him what we wanted and then ordered some drinks, a Margarita for Suzy, Screwdriver for me.

After a few minutes, the waiter brought us our drinks.

"So, tell me about yourself, Brent."

"Oh, you don't want to know about me; it's so dull. I want to know all about you."

"Like what?"

"I don't know where were you born to start?"

"That's going back a long way...but if that's what you want to know. I was born in Hong Kong, and I came over here when I was two with my Parents. They bought that building and restaurant you were in tonight. I grew up in the city. I've never been back to Hong Kong except when I was about ten or so to see some relatives."

"Have you always worked in the restaurant?"

"Yes. I practically grew up there. I love it. Someday it'll be mine. Have you known Alex and Maggie long?"

"For a while now. I've known Alex as far back as basic training. We trained together in Texas. We both ended up in the same unit and got shipped to Saigon. He met Maggie there within the first year. It was love at first sight. Before he met her, we used to hang out together. You know we would go out drinking and partying. Of course, all that changed when he met Maggie. When I first met her, Alex had been out with her twice. He introduced us out at the Base Cantina. They were having a drink together, and I walked in. They looked so happy together, and they had been going out for about a year or so. Then things started to change."

"What do you mean, change?"

"I don't know, Alex started drinking heavily and had trouble showing up for work. It was about that time I got discharged and sent back to the States. I lost track of them until he called me the other day to tell me Maggie was missing. That's all I know right now.

"Hey, let's not talk about them. Tell me something about you."

"There isn't much to tell; I own my own Private Investigation Agency."

"Have you always had the agency?"

"No. I started it about three years ago. Before that, I was an Assistant Vice President of a big Insurance Company uptown."

"Why did you leave?"

"I got lucky, the chance came for me to leave and go into business for myself and I took it. I found out working for a large company like that can be very hard on your health."

"What do you mean?"

"They play a lot of games within the employees and upper management. I didn't need it, nor did I like it."

The waiter came and brought us our food. We started to eat; there wasn't much said until we finished. I'll say one thing about Suzy; she could sure put the food away. I don't know how she kept that slim figure she had. After dinner, we ordered another drink.

Suzie looked at me kind of strangely and said, "Are you married?"

I had to laugh because of the way she looked when she asked, "What made you ask that question? Do I look married?

"I don't know for a minute you had the look of a man that was married; that's all."

"Well, no, I'm not. What about you?"

"Oh no, I'm too young, the state of New York wouldn't let me without permission from my parents."

"Right, I should have seen that right away when I saw you sitting at your bar looking like Cinderella." We both laughed.

I reached across the table and held her hand while I stared at those beautifully shaped almonds' eyes. They look like pools of black ink. It was almost like looking into a bottomless pool of endlessness.

"Brent, are you okay?"

"Uh...a... sure."

"What were you thinking?"

"How pretty you are, and I was wondering how it would feel to kiss you."

As I talked, I leaned across the table and kissed her. I was waiting for her to move back and stop me, but she didn't.

Afterward, she looked at me, smiled, and said, "Well...Were you disappointed?"

I was speechless. Suzy's lips were so soft they felt like the petals of a rose.

I just stared at her for a moment and then said, "No, not at all."

"Good, now what would you like for dessert?"

She started laughing, and I said, "Your kidding, aren't you?"

"Yes, I'm kidding. It's getting late, and I must get up early tomorrow. I'm a working girl, you know. Would you mind taking me home?"

"Yeah, I better take you home, but it's against my better judgment."

She smiled and put her hand on my face again and said, "I know, but there'll be another time."

Then she looked serious and said, "There will be won't there?"

"You bet."

"Good, C'mon."

I took Suzy back to her restaurant and dropped her off at her car. Then I watched Suzy leave to make sure she got off okay. Then I headed home for the night.

CHAPTER TWO

The morning came too fast. I didn't sleep too well last night. I kept thinking about Lily and what she had to do with all of this. Not to mention the fact I got hit on the head in her apartment. I don't know who it was, nor do I know where Lily is at this moment.

When I got to the office, Vera told me Bill Singer was on the line, and he sounded upset.

"Vera, do me a favor, find out what you can about a Lily Carter alias 'Lily the cabbie.' I'll take the call in my office."

I went into my office and sat for a moment behind my desk to get my composure, knowing why Bill had called. He probably discovered he had a picture of Maggie in his missing person report. It matched the description he found on Sammy. I picked up the phone and tried to sound pleasant. I put him on the speakerphone.

"Good morning, Bill, how are you?"

"Don't good morning me, you son of a bitch. Why didn't you tell me you knew the girl in the picture I showed you was Maggie?"

"Now wait a minute, listen to what I'm about to tell you."

"Go ahead, I'm listening, and it better be good."

"Your right, I did know that was Maggie, but I wanted to talk to Alex before you. He would be more apt to talk to me than you."

"Okay, smartass, what did you find out that I couldn't?"

"Nothing, much except that a couple of months ago, Alex's' apartment was broken into, they took some of his pictures,"

"No money. Just pictures?"

"Yes."

"That doesn't make any sense."

"I know, it didn't make any sense to Alex and Maggie, either that's why they didn't report it to the police."

"That's just great; I'm right back where I started."

"Not quite, Bill."

"What do you mean?"

"I think Sammy broke into their apartment and took the pictures because I had asked him if he had heard anything about her and to find out what he could. He probably wanted a picture to ask around with; We also know that Maggie is involved in this up to her pretty little neck, also that Sammy could have, been killed because of it. A week before he was found dead, Sammy told me that a coke deal went down in Brooklyn concerning the Rizzio brothers. The money was stolen before the brothers could get their hands on it. Now maybe, just maybe it's all connected in some way."

"That doesn't leave me very much to go on, Brent."

"No, but let me consider it, and I'll get back to you on it, okay?"

"Okay, but if you blow this one, the Captain is going to have my badge, and I'm going to have your ass, Understood?"

"Don't worry about a thing, oh, and Bill check on a Lily Carter. She may have been the last person to see Sammy alive, and she has disappeared."

"Just remember what I said and stay in touch."

I got Vera on the intercom and told her to have my Rx7 downstairs in five minutes. I was going to see Janie again.

Maybe she could shed some light on why Lily's disappeared. Sammy might have had a chance to tell her something before he went for that permanent swim.

It was lunchtime when I arrived at Joe's. I had forgotten how crowded it gets at that time of the day. I was about to leave and come back later when I saw this young woman sitting with a couple of older men. She dressed like a cabbie, but somehow, she didn't fit in. I was curious, so I decided to stick around and find out how she fits in.

Janie saw me come in and waved for me to come over. She was at her usual place behind the bar at the other end. She was talking to a few of the customers. I went over.

"Hi, Janie, how's it going?"

"Well, Brent, you're getting to be a steady customer these days."

"It's your charm, Janie; it's irresistible."

"That's what I like about you, Brent; you always tell me what I like to hear. What's up?"

"Can we go where it's a little less public? I've got a couple of questions to ask you about Sammy and Lily."

"Sure, c'mon follow me, there's a quiet booth over here."

She led me to a booth in the back part of the bar, where there were fewer people.

"Now, what's on your mind?"

"When was the last time you saw Sammy alive?"

"Let's see...That would have been last Monday. Yeah, Monday, why?"

"Well, did he say anything to you that would give you the impression he might be in danger?"

"He did say something that sounded a little strange."

"What was that?"

"Sammy said he was doing some snooping for you and was glad he had finished it because he had the feeling all day that someone was following him. He said he got so scared at one point that Sammy wrote down the information he found out. Then mailed it to you in case he didn't make it."

"Did you tell this to the police?"

"Nah, you know me, I don't talk to no flat foot."

"Janie, they don't call them flatfoots anymore."

"You call them what you want. I call police flatfoots."

"What about Lily?"

"Now, there's a strange one for you. Lilly's been coming in here for the last five months, never talked to anyone except Sammy. Then the day before they discovered Sammy's body, in the river she calls me. Says she has to find a place to hide."

"Hide, from who, why?"

"I don't know; she didn't tell me any more than that."

"What did you tell her?"

"I told her I had this friend of mine she could stay a few days with, and he lived in Elmont. That's out near Belmont racetrack."

"Yeah, I know the place. Why didn't you tell me this before I went to Lily's apartment and nearly got my head knocked off?"

"Well, I made a promise to Lily that I wouldn't."

"Great, can I have the address now?"

"Sure, no problem."

She started to write down the address while I turned and looked at that young-looking cabbie. Maggie handed the paper to me and saw me staring at the women.

"Like that, huh?"

"Yeah, she's attractive, who is she?"

"You're not going to believe this, but she's Sammy's daughter. She's been away at school. When Sammy showed up dead, we found her address when we were going through his things. We called and told her what had happened."

"Interesting, what's her name?"

"Laura, want me to introduce her to you?"

"No, that's okay. I can do that, thanks."

I walked up to her; she was sitting with a couple of cabbies. She looked to be about twenty-four or so. Not beautiful, but there was something about her that made her very attractive. She stood about five-foot-four with short black hair and green eyes. I said hello; she looked up at me with a puzzled look on her face.

"Hello, do I know you?"

"Not really, I was a friend of your fathers. My name is Brent Stewart."

"Oh yes, you're that private investigator that drives around with a female chauffeur. My father mentioned you to me; I'm Laura Wilson."

"Yes, I know. Do you mind if we talk alone for a few minutes?"

"No, not at all." Then looking at the cabbies, she said, "Guys, do you mind?"

As they got up to leave, I sat down next to her and waved at Janie for a beer.

"Can I get you something?"

"Well, I don't drink, but you can get me a Pepsi."

When Janie brought me my beer, I told her to bring Laura a Pepsi.

"Tell me, Ms. Wilson, did your father ever mention a woman named Lily to you?"

"Please, call me Laura. You mean, Lily, the cabbie?"

"Yes."

"Sure, they've been living together since my mother died, four years now."

"I knew Sammy for almost a year before he died, and he never mentioned that to me."

"He didn't want anyone to know about their relationship."

She saw the look of puzzlement on my face and went on to explain.

"You know, everybody knew Sammy ran a newsstand. He was also an informer on the side, and he never tried to hide it. He didn't want to put Lily in danger, so he tried to keep his relationship with her a secret."

"How many people knew about it?"

"As far as I know, only me and Mousey."

"Do you know Lilies last name?"

"Dad never told me. We just called her Lily, the cabbie."

"Before your father died, he was working on something for me. Did he ever mention it to you?"

"No. Dad didn't like to worry me, which is why he sent me away to college. That way, I was out of the danger myself, and he didn't have to worry about me. I always hated him for that."

"Why was that?"

"Ever since mom died, he's shut me out of his life. He was afraid I wouldn't survive in his world. It was as if he wanted to keep me safe in a bottle. Out of harm's way, sort of speak."

"Have you heard from Lily since your father died?"

"No, and it bothers me that after my father was found dead, she disappeared. The owner of this bar, Janie, got in touch with me at school to tell me what had happened. So, I rushed back here."

"Well, there isn't much to go on, but I'm following every lead that comes up. I'm sure we'll find Lily; it's just a matter of time."

"Thank you, Mr. Stewart. I appreciate everything you're doing. I want to help if I could."

"If I can call you Laura, then, by all means, call me Brent. It isn't much you can do at this point. The wife of an old friend of mine is missing. I had asked Sammy to keep his eyes and ears open in case something came up. To notify me, and I would take care of the rest."

"If you need me, I'll be running my father's newsstand until I can sell it and get back to school. Now, if you'll excuse me, I must be going."

"Of course, Laura. Thank you for your time."

I watched as Laura left Joes'. She seems to have it together. Although, she didn't seem too broken up about her father's death. Well, it was getting late, and I wanted to get out to Elmont and check out that address Janie gave me. As I left, I turned and waved to Janie, saying, see you later.

As I headed for the car, I looked at the address she gave me. It was the home of a Mr. Topo, on Endor Street.

I got in my car and headed out to the Long Island Expressway. One thing about New York, when they take on a project it seems to take forever; at least it felt that way. As far back as I could remember, they've been working on the L.I.E. They call this the 'City of Bridges.' It should be called the city of projects. The traffic was starting to get busy as I headed toward Elmont. I got off the Belmont exit and pulled into a gas station. A kid was attending the pumps. I went up to him and asked him if he knew where Endor Street was.

"Sure, Mister, you go about three blocks down that way and make a left. That's Whitsett, then you make a left and go two blocks. That's Endor."

"Thanks, here's a couple of bucks."

I got back in the car and headed out. I've always liked Long Island; it reminded me of a beautiful, friendly place where people cared. As I approached Endor, there were some kids playing stickball. That's a game you play with a broomstick handle as a bat and a rubber ball. It sure brought back a lot of memories watching them play. I pulled up in front of the address Janie had given me. I got out, went to the door, and knocked.

After a few minutes, an older man answered. He was short and bald and had a pipe in his mouth. He looked to be about sixty or so.

"Can I help you, mister?"

"Yes, I'm a friend of Janie's, and I'm looking for a woman named Lily. She said I could find her here."

"Just a minute."

He closed the door, and he left for about a minute or so. When the door opened again, Lily was standing there. I knew it was Lily because I remember seeing her with Sammy at Joe's.

"What do you want?"

"Hi, Lily. I was a friend of Sammy's; I'd like to talk to you if I may."

"Who sent you here?"

"Janie told me you would be here. Can I come in for a few minutes?"

She opened the door and told me to come in. She showed me to the living room and asked if I wanted some coffee. It was one of those old homes they don't make anymore. The house's today, they put them up so fast you wonder if they're as sturdy as the old ones. I like the old ones better. This one had a beautiful fireplace on one side of the living room. You could tell the person that lived here had been alone for a long time. It had that lived-in look.

"No, thank you, Lily. I won't take up much of your time."

"Ok, then why don't you at least sit down." Pointing to the couch, on the other side of the room.

I went over and sat down.

"I have a few questions for you. My name is Brent Stewart; I'm a private investigator."

"Oh yes, I heard Sammy talk about you plenty of times. He liked you. He used to say when he got rich, Sammy wanted to hire a female chauffeur as you had. He was funny that way."

"Tell me, Lily, why did you disappear after Sammy showed up dead?

She started to get a little nervous as she talked. She paced back and forth across the room.

"After you spoke to Sammy that day in Joe's, he started snooping around. I told him not to get involved that it could be dangerous. He would laugh it off and say, 'Lily, this could be the one to get me out of the city.'

"Out of the city?"

"Yes, Sammy wanted to move to the Jersey shore but never had the money. He figured, if he could score big, he could move. Sammy was always dreaming' like that. It was one of the things I loved about him. He loved life and living."

Lily started crying, and I went over and put my arms around her. I told her to sit down.

"I'll be all right. Mr. Stewart, are you sure I couldn't get you something?"

"No, thank you."

"Well, I'm going to have a drink."

She got up and went to the kitchen. She came back with a bottle of Scotch and a glass of water. She took a swig of the scotch and a sip of the water.

"That's better. I'm sorry; I promised myself I wouldn't cry anymore."

"That's okay. You go right ahead. Lily, why did you go to my friend's place in Chinatown?"

"Sammy gave me a note in an envelope. He said for me to tack it on the door and leave."

"Did you know what the note said?"

"No, Sammy said he got it from a friend, and he had to go someplace in a hurry. Then he asked me to deliver it. I was supposed to see him later that night, but he never showed up."

"Did he say where he got the note or who gave it to him?"

"No, he just said we would get five hundred dollars if we delivered the note, so I did. That was the last time I saw Sammy."

She sat there, considering the glass-like her whole world was hiding right there.

"Thanks, Lily. I know how hard this is for you. If I need you, I know where I can reach you."

"I guess you can reach me here. I don't have any place to go, so I'll stay in hiding for a while."

I left and headed back to the city. It was dinner time, and I was getting a little hungry. I stopped at a restaurant outside of Elmont and got something to eat. It was times like these I wished I were in another business. Sometimes you can help someone, and that's the delicate part of this business. Other times, life's a bitch, and there is nothing you can do no matter how hard you try.

I arrived back in the city around seven, and I was exhausted. I went straight back to my apartment. That's one of the pleasant things about having a lot of money. You can have your business and home in the same building. They've been reconstructing and remodeling the old buildings on the Upper East Side.

A few years ago, I bought the top two floors in an office building on the Upper East Side. The top-level had a penthouse on it. I use that as my residence and the floor below that as a business office.

Johnny, the security guard, had been with the building for ten years now. He was in his forties and is married with two kids. He greeted me as I came up from the parking lot to the building.

"Good evening, Mr. Stewart."

"Good evening, Johnny. How was your day?"

"Pretty good, Mr. Stewart. My boy Steve had to get braces today. He didn't care much for that."

"No, I don't suppose he did. He'll get over it, and he'll thank you for it in a few years.

"Yep, that's for sure."

"Goodnight, Johnny."

"Good night, Mr. Stewart."

I headed for the penthouse elevator and took it to the top. There is only one elevator that goes straight to the Penthouse; it's my private entrance. It was going to feel good to take a nice hot shower and have a drink before turning in. One of the things I loved about the city was looking at it at night with all its shimmering lights. Looking from my balcony, I could see both sides of the town, the East River, and the Hudson River. Looking downtown, I could see the Empire State building and further down, more business districts, Wall Street area. On a clear night, I could see the Statue of Liberty and the sparkling lights on Staten Island. Looking cross-town, I could see the pitch black of Central Park.

The lights in the park lit a trail all through it that gave it a serene feeling. You could see car headlights as they made their way through the park going from the East Side to the West Side. It was the time of the day I liked best about my city. People were getting ready to call it a day. Some had already done so. It was peaceful from a distance you could hear taxi horns and buses. I like to call it the sounds of the city. Every so often, you could listen to an

Ambulance or a Police car, and I knew there was trouble in my back yard. I couldn't solve all the problems in my city, but at least I could help. I guess that's what it's all about. I finished my drink and hit the sack.

CHAPTER THREE

I left word with Johnny to have Vera wake me at ten; it came fast. I guess I was more tired than I thought. When I heard the phone ring once, I picked it up, and I heard Millie saying Mr. Stewart's residence. I told Millie I'd take it. Millie had been with me five years now. Millie was the housekeeper and cook. She only lived about three blocks away in one of those old brownstones. Her husband left the place to her when he died a few years back. I tried to get her to move in here permanently, but she wouldn't have it. She said she would feel like a kept woman.

I heard Vera's' voice at the other end of the phone. "Good morning, Vera, what's up?"

"Sorry to bother you, Brent, but it's ten o'clock, and you did leave a wake up for ten."

"No problem, Vera I'll be down in about an hour, in the meantime do me a favor, will you? Get all the information you can on the Lawyer Maggie used to work for before she disappeared."

"Right, Brent. Anything else?"

"Yes, have Alex meet me in the office at eleven-thirty this morning."

"Okay, is that all?"

"Yes."

I hung up and went in and took a shower when I came out Millie had breakfast ready for me. The smell of fresh bacon and eggs and coffee with hot toast makes the start of my day worthwhile.

When I got downstairs, Vera had the information I requested on my desk. The folder had the names Todd, Williams, and Brady Inc. as the name of the company where Maggie worked. Interesting background on the firm, they are all brothers. Why the different last names you say. Well, their mother was married three different times. She had a son by each husband, Mr. Todd, Mr. Williams, and Mr. Brady. The mother comes from a fascinating family, also. Her maiden name was Castellano of the infamous Castellano family of Queens, one of the higher-ups in the Mafia family in the city. Things were starting to get real interesting. The Head of the family was using her maiden name again. She was no longer married to Mr. Brady. Mr. Brady was no longer of this world. Mr. Brady disappeared about a year ago; the word has it; he dropped out of favor with the family. His body was sleeping with the fishes somewhere in the East River. They never found his body.

Michael Brady, the youngest of the three sons, just passed the bar. He had only been in the family business for a year. Sonny Williams pulled some strings with the family so he wouldn't have to attend that little party they had in Viet Nam. He had better things to do, like finishing law school. Jack Todd, the oldest, started the business in the early sixties. He is the most enterprising of the three and the most dangerous.

The leader of the family, Mama Castellano, has been running the family businesses since her father was gunned down outside a restaurant in Brooklyn back in fifty-five. They never did find the killers. It was in all the papers at the time. Rumor has it that a family from Chicago was trying to move in on the Castellanos. They didn't make it. The word around town right now is that the sons disagree with Mama Castellano.

The sons want to keep the drug trade with some Chinese connections out of Hong Kong. Mama, on the other hand, doesn't want to deal with the stuff. She doesn't approve of kids using the drugs and then having the kids overdose on it, so much for American motherhood.

Vera buzzed me on the intercom to tell me that Alex was waiting outside. I told her to show him in.

"Alex, how's it going, old buddy? Come in and sit down." Alex looked like he hadn't slept for a couple of days. He started pacing back and forth like a caged lion.

"Brent, have you got any news of Maggie?"

"Take it easy, Alex, sit down. I have some questions to ask you?" Alex sat down but still couldn't keep his feet quite. He started doing that nervous tapping on the floor. It was annoying me, but I guess he had a right to be worried and upset.

"Well, first, I want to tell you we haven't heard anything about Maggie. We haven't given up. We've got a few leads to work on, tell me, Alex, did Maggie ever talk to you about her work?"

"No, I know she enjoyed working for the firm."

"Did Maggie ever come home with some of the work, or discuss any work from the office?"

"No, she did say they were getting a bigger office and would probably have to hire some more secretaries. She said they told her she would be their number one secretary in charge of the office."

"Did you know that the firm belonged to the Castellano family of Queens?"

"No, I didn't."

"Okay, I guess that will be all, Alex. Don't worry about anything. If I hear anything, I'll be sure to let you know. Do yourself a favor and get some sleep, you look like shit."

"I will; you won't forget to call me if you hear anything?"

"I said I would call if anything comes up, and I will now go."

After Alex had left, I called up Suzy and asked her if she would like to have dinner at my place tonight. She said, yes and I told her my car would pick her up at five o'clock this evening. I called Vera and told her to have my car downstairs in five minutes.

I wanted to pay a visit to the law firm of Todd, Williams, and Brady and have a little chat with them.

Mama Castellano owns among others, a beautiful building on West Forty-ninth Street just off Park Ave. The law firm of Todd, Williams, and Brady is on the first two floors of the building.

As I went inside, I couldn't help thinking, being on the first two floors of the building makes it convenient if they must get out of the building in a hurry. There was an attractive middle-aged woman at the front desk.

"May I be of some help?"

"Yes, I'd like to see Mr. Todd."

"Do you have an appointment?"

"No, I don't."

"Who shall I say is here?"

"My name is Brent Stewart of the 'Stewart Investigative Agency.'"

"Thank you, sir. Mr. Stewart, if you will please have a seat over there. I'll tell him you are here. Oh, by the way, what is this concerning?"

"The disappearance of one of his employees, Mrs. Lomax's."

She looked at me with the look of a person that was sorry she asked. I shook my shoulders at her and went over and sat on the office couch. A few minutes later, a man about five-ten or so came walking out of his office. He had broad shoulders. I could see right away where a woman would find him very attractive.

The secretary spoke, "Mr. Stewart, this is Mr. Todd."

I shook his hand and said, "How are you, Mr. Todd, may I have a few words with you in private?"

"Mr. Stewart, won't you come into my office."

As we walked into his office, I could see it was unmistakably Italian. There was a bronze statue of Rodin's 'The Thinker' sitting on a pedestal.

There were also some pictures on the wall that was distinctively Italian. Mr. Todd asked me to sit; I did.

"Well, Mr. Stewart, how can I help you?"

"Mr. Todd, when was the last time you saw Mrs. Lomax?"

"Let's see...two weeks ago yesterday. Mrs. Lomax asked me if she could have her two weeks' vacation early. She said she received a letter from her father in San Francisco and had to take care of some personal business. Of course, I said yes."

"Did she seem nervous or upset?"

"Come to think of it, she did. I asked her if there was something, I could take care of for her; she thanked me and declined my offer. That was it."

"And that was the last time you saw her?"

"Yes."

Just then, the door swung open and in walked this man. He looked to be about twenty-five or so. He didn't wait to come all the way in before he started to talk.

"Jack, listen, I just got a call from that china man on the coast."

Before he could say anything, else Mister Todd interrupted him.

"Er...Sonny, this is Mr. Stewart, he's investigating the disappearance of Maggie."

Sonny looked at me like he almost said something he wasn't supposed to say and stopped in time.

"Oh, how are you, Mr. Stewart. I'm sorry to interrupt. Jack, I'd like to talk to you in my office when you're finished."

"If you don't have any more questions for me, Mister Stewart. I do have some business to attend."

"No, I guess that'll be all for now."

I got up and started to leave when Mr. Todd spoke.

"Mr. Stewart, please let us know if you find out anything. We are concerned about Maggie. She is one of our best workers, and we would hate to lose her."

Something was telling me that Mr. Todd wasn't sincere, but I couldn't put my finger on it.

"Thank you, and you have a good day, Mr. Todd."

As I left, Mr. Todd shut the door. I walked past the secretary's desk, and she handed me a note. I looked at her, and she looked back down at her typing as I walked out. I got back in the car and told Maxine to take me back to the office. As I sat in the car, I read the note. It read, 'I'll be home in an hour, call me.' She had her phone number written at the bottom, along with her name, Susan Scotto.

When I got back to my office, I had a visitor I didn't expect, the Godmother herself. I knew it was her because I had seen her picture in the paper a few times in the last five years. A person of her caliber manages to get her photo taken a few times.

"How are you, Mrs. Castellano, won't you come into my office?"

"Yes, thank you."

I showed her in and asked if she would like some coffee.

"No, but if you have some wine, I'd like a glass."

I called Vera on the intercom and told her to bring in two glasses of wine.

Mrs. Castellano was a woman of statue grace and charm. You could also tell by looking at her that you wouldn't want to get on her wrong side. She was about five feet, three inches tall. The years had treated her well, considering the business she was in for so many years.

"Mr. Stewart, I understand you're investigating the disappearance of Mrs. Maggie Lomax."

"Why, yes, but how does that concern you?"

"It doesn't."

She stopped talking as Vera entered the room with the drinks.

"Thank you, Vera, that'll be all."

Vera turned and left. I looked at Mrs. Castellano as she took a sip of the wine.

"You were saying, Mrs. Castellano."

"Yes, I was saying that it was of no concern of mine. Only I didn't want the family name involved in this. As you know, I have a reputation to watch."

"You don't have to watch it. Everybody else is doing that for you."

"That's exactly what I'm talking about."

"Yes, well now, all I'm interested in is finding the wife of an old friend of mine. If that means stepping on a few toes, I'm sorry."

Mrs. Castellano stood up and looked at me with a look that seemed to say, don't rattle my cage; you may not like what drops out. Then she turned around and walked out without saying a word leaving the door open. Vera stuck her head in just before closing it, smiled, and gave me the old okay sign. Then she shut the door. I sat there for a moment, thinking about what just had happened. I wondered if maybe I might have bitten off a little bit more than I could chew. I had the feeling I would be hearing from Mama Castellano again very soon. I decided to call Mr. Todd's secretary and see what she had to say. The phone rang three times before someone answered.

"Hello, Ms. Scotto?"

"Mrs. Scotto, yes, who is this?"

"My name is Brent Stewart, and I met you at Mr. Todd's office today. You asked me to call you at home."

"Oh yes, well, we can't talk right now. I'm off tomorrow, could I meet you outside the Museum of Natural History tomorrow at noon, we can talk then?"

"That'll be fine, Mrs. Scotto. I look forward to seeing you then. Good day."

I walked out of the office, telling Vera I was going to call it a day. Unless it's an emergency, don't disturb me. I am going upstairs and relaxing in the Jacuzzi for a while. I told Millie there would be two for dinner tonight.

"What would you like to have, Mr. Stewart?"

"How about some Prime Rib and Baked Potatoes with some red wine?"

"Yes, Mr. Stewart."

"If you think of anything else that would be nice, add it."

"Yes, Mr. Stewart. What time would you like dinner served?"

"Well, she'll be here about five-thirty, so let's make it six. That way, you can get home early."

As I stepped into the Jacuzzi and relaxed, I was reminded of how lucky I was to have one of these in my apartment. There weren't too many people in New York City with them. I stayed in it a little longer than I wanted to. When I looked at my watch, it was four forty-five. I climbed out and started to get dressed. Just as I finished and was putting on my sports coat, the front doorbell rang. I told Millie I would get it and went to the door and opened it.

There stood Suzy in an evening dress that would make an older man feel young again or at least wish he were.

"C' mon in; you look beautiful."

Suzy walked in, looked around, turned, and said, "You know if I'd had known you lived here, I would have looked you up sooner."

I just looked at her and smiled while saying, "I like to call it home."

"Right honey, you call it home, I'll call it a palace."

"Millie almost has dinner ready."

"Millie, don't tell me. She's your cook and housekeeper."

"Yes, how did you know?"

She laughed and said, "Oh, a lucky guess."

We both laughed and went into the dining room, where we sat down for dinner. Millie brought out glasses of wine for both of us and left.

"Do you always entertain your guests this way?"

"Just the special ones, shall we toast?"

"What shall we toast to?"

"How about an interesting evening with a special person who's been on my mind all day."

"Anybody, I know?"

"No, my Mother."

Suzy laughed, and we touched glasses and drank. Suzy got up with her glass and walked over to the patio and looked out.

"This place is not to be believed. How long have you had this place?"

"Going on five years."

"Mind if we take a tour?"

"No, of course not. Follow me."

First, I took her to the study, then the living room.

"I love this living room. Did you decorate yourself?"

"No, I had someone come in and do it for me."

"Very nice."

Next, I showed her the bedroom and the Jacuzzi. The bedroom had a big round bed in the center on a platform, which rotated with buttons. There were mirrors on the ceiling. There were blue see-thru drapes around the bed.

"Well, I must say you know how to live."

She looked at me and started to say something and then stopped. Just then, Millie entered the room and said dinner was ready. We went back to the dining room to eat. After dinner, we went out on the patio to have a drink and to look over the city.

"This is my favorite place to be at night when I want to think about the events of the day."

"Oh, Brent, it's beautiful, look, there's Central Park, and over there is the Empire State Building, the lights look so beautiful."

"Yeah, that's one of the reasons I bought this place. I love the view from here."

Just then, Millie came out with some wine for us.

"Mr. Stewart, I'm finished inside, so I'm going home for the night if that's okay with you."

"Sure, go ahead, Millie. I left word with Maxine downstairs to take you home, and then Maxine could close her night out too."

"Fine, I'll see you on Thursday."

As Millie turned and left, Suzy turned to me and said, "Boy, you sure do know how to live."

"Yeah, well, it's one of the nice things about being rich. Now, where were we?"

"You were telling me the view was one of the reasons you bought this place."

"Ah, yes, way up here, it is peaceful above the city."

I moved close to Suzy and kissed her on the lips. They were as soft as silk sheets on a bed.

"Hmmm, that was nice. What do you do for an encore?"

"This. Suzy said."

As she said that she moved even closer and slowly put her arms around me and kissed me. It was intense and passionate, and suddenly, I remembered what I liked about the Asian woman. I picked her up and carried her to the bedroom and laid her down on the bed.

She looked up at me and said, "I didn't say yes."

"Yes, you did with your eyes."

She smiled and put her hands up to me and pulled me down. Our bodies met and got to know each other well. As I ran my hand over her beautiful body, I could feel the silk of the dress. It felt as if the rest of the world had disappeared, almost like it felt guilty, it had intruded on us. As I kissed her on the neck, I heard her say, wait a minute. She undid her dress and took it off. All she had under it was a pair of black panties. She laid back down as I took off my shirt and pants. We embraced again, and her hands were all over my body as we caressed each other. We were preparing each other for a night of passion. Awakening all the nerves in our bodies and telling them to run wild and then reacting to the desires, with our bodies.

As morning came, I awoke to the sweet smell of breakfast. Before I could get out of bed, Suzy came walking in with my robe on. She had a tray of coffee, eggs, bacon, and toast.

"What are you doing?"

"Well, you were so good to me last night I thought I'd be good to you this morning."

I smiled and said, "Come here, I want more of last night."

She put the tray down and lay on top of me and kissed me good morning. Just then, the phone rang when I answered it. It was Vera downstairs.

"Hello. Yes, yes, all right; I'll be down in a bit, tell the messenger to wait."

I turned to Suzie, "I'm sorry, honey, business. I have a visitor downstairs, I should see. Why don't you get dressed and let yourself out, and I'll call you tonight, okay?"

"But, Brent."

"I'm sorry, Honey."

I got up and went into the shower and shaved and got ready. As I left to go downstairs, Suzy was still pouting, I felt terrible, but when Mama Castellano sends one of her messengers over, you see them.

As I entered the office, he was sitting there waiting for me. He had a business suit on, and he spoke very well. I mean, he sounded educated.

"Mr. Stewart?"

"Yes, can I help you?"

"Can we go into your office?"

"Of course, follow me."

I went into the office and sat behind my desk. I told my visitor to relax, but the messenger didn't want to.

"This won't take long. Mama Castellano asked me to tell you that Maggie's father is the cause of the disappearance. If you talk to him in San Francisco, he could tell you everything."

"Did Mama Castellano give you his phone number too?"

"No, she said you were resourceful and that you could find that out yourself, but he probably wouldn't answer."

"Why not?"

"Well, sir, I was told to tell you that if you went to San Francisco, you would find out."

"Thank you for the information. Anything else?"

"No."

He turned and walked out of the office. I walked out to see Vera.

"Vera, call Mike at Linden Airport and tell him to get the Jet ready. I want him to fly me to San Francisco this afternoon. Tell him to be ready to take off when I get there at two o'clock. Vera, what time is it in San Francisco now?"

"Let's see; there is three hours difference, so that means it's eleven o'clock in the morning San Francisco time."

"Good, perfect. Tell Mike, and we'll leave at two our time."

I went upstairs to pack, and Suzy was still there.

"I thought you would have been out of here by now."

"Well, Brent, I was on my way out, but now that you're here, I'm not so sure."

She walked up to me and put her arms around me and kissed me. I thought, oh well, I've got plenty of time. Besides, I liked the way Suzy kissed, and it had a relaxing effect on me. Then I remembered an appointment I had with Mrs. Scotto.

"Sorry kid, I have to go see another woman about a note."

"What do you mean?"

I laughed and said, "Don't worry, it's just a secretary I met yesterday. It has to do with the case I'm on."

"Oh, okay. I should be going anyway."

Suzy turned and left. I went to the phone and called Ms. Scotto and told her I would meet her at the Museum in thirty minutes. She said, okay.

When I arrived, she was standing on the steps. She told me she was just recently married and loved her job with the firm.

"Why did you want to talk to me?"

"Well, yesterday in Mr. Todd's office, I overheard you talking to Mr. Todd about Maggie."

"Yes!"

"Well, I spoke to Maggie about two days before she disappeared, and she told me she had received this letter from her father in San Francisco, and she sounded apprehensive. When I asked her if I could help, she snapped at me. That's not like her; she was usually very calm and polite.

I don't know if it means anything, but she told me she had to go to San Francisco to see her father. She said he was in trouble."

"What else did she say?"

"Nothing really, it was more the way she was acting. Mr. Stewart, you won't tell Mr. Todd I talked to you, will you? I mean, it could mean my job."

"Don't worry, Susan. You can be sure this never happened. If you hear anything that you think might help me, let me know, okay?"

"Sure thing Mr. Stewart, I better go now."

She left, and I headed back to the apartment to pack. I was taking Mr. Horace Greeley's advice and going west.

Chapter Four

Michael, my pilot, has been with me since the beginning. I hired him the same time I hired Maxine. I like having my Jet. It's handy; besides, I love flying. When I was in the service, I took lessons and continued them when I got out. I'm certified and fly whenever I can.

Right now, I wanted to do some thinking about this case. Michael used to fly in Nam after he got out, he took odd jobs flying for private companies. I bumped into him at David Copperfield's on the East Side.

That's a Restaurant I used to frequent from time to time. They have great food there.

I have a bad feeling about this case. I took the address of Mr. Chong from the letters that Alex gave me. What worried me was that Mama Castellano was helping. I don't want to have to take on the family. I try to stay away from those cases. I didn't know what I was going to find when I got to San Francisco. Whatever it was, I had a feeling it wasn't going to be good.

The flight plans we filed said we would arrive at San Francisco Airport at about three-thirty in the afternoon California time. That sounds funny since we left Linden Airport at two in the afternoon. The time zones are what make the difference.

I had Vera phone ahead and have a car ready for me at the Airport when I arrived. The weather was typically California for this time of the day. The fog had already lifted over the Golden Gate Bridge when we arrived.

After we landed, I told Michael to meet me here tomorrow at about five p.m. I figured that would be time enough to find out everything I needed. Michael said he knew a girl in San Francisco he hasn't seen in a long time and he was going to give her a call.

Vera made reservations for me at the Holiday Inn down by Fisherman's Wharf, so I headed there. I checked in and got squared away. Then I checked the phone book for a phone number under Mr. Chong's name with the address that was on the envelope. Do you know how many Chong's there are in San Francisco, a whole bunch? Anyway, I didn't find one I wanted. So, I took a ride over to the address Vera had given me. It was in the middle of Chinatown. I expected no less. The address was between a coffee shop and a little shop that sold Buddha statues. I went inside, and the building reminded me of the old cold-water flats in New York. Except these were kept in much better shape.

I went upstairs and knocked on number seven. There was no answer. I started to leave when two big Chinese men came up to me and asked me what I wanted with Mr. Chong. I guess it was the way I answered them that they didn't like. The taller gentleman pulled out a gun and told me to go with them. At this point, I wasn't going to argue.

When we got downstairs, they took me outside in the back alley and asked me again. I asked them who wants to know that's when the shorter one hit me, and I kissed the ground. Before I could get up, the other gentleman kicked me. I heard one of them say if I found Mr. Chong, I was to give him a message for them.

They kept hitting me, as the lights started going out, I heard one of them saying, 'Tell Mr. Chong he can't hide from us.'

When I woke up, it was dark, and a cat had just jumped over me and headed for a turned over trash can next to me. My head felt like; it had been used as a battering ram for a door. I picked myself up, very slowly and straightened my clothes, and headed for the car. I looked at my watch; it was about six. I headed back to the hotel to call Vera.

I walked into the hotel lobby and went up to the desk clerk to get my key. He looked at me like I was a bum.

"Excuse me, sir, but can I help you?"

"Yes, I would like to have the key to my room, please."

He looked at me, unbelievingly, and said, "Your room, sir?"

"Yes, my name is Brent Stewart. I'm in room 506. You'll have to excuse me; I tripped and fell in one of your trash cans outside."

"Of course, sir, here's your key. Now, if you'll be so kind as to tell me which can it was, I'll have it emptied so it won't happen again."

I smiled and said, "Won't be necessary. I did it already."

"Excellent, sir."

I turned and headed for the elevator. On the way up, my head kept reminding me of those two guys, and I was hoping to see them again, only on my terms.

When I got to my room, I took a nice hot shower and put a call through to Vera. I told the operator downstairs to ring me up when she got through. My timing was perfect just as I got out of the shower and dried myself off the phone rang.

"Hello, yes, put it through an operator. Hello Vera, yes, everything is okay. I just ran into the welcome wagon. I don't think they like tourists in this town very much. No, I'm fine. Listen, did you hear anything from Maggie yet. Okay, I should be home tomorrow night. It looks like I ran into a dead-end out here; see you then bye."

After I hung up, I decided my body had enough excitement for one day, and it was time to hit the sack. I must have been asleep for only a few hours when there was a knock on my door. I got up and went to the door. When I opened it, there stood an old Chinese woman. I asked her in and asked what she wanted.

"Excuse me, sir, for disturbing you, but I saw those two men take you outside in the alley at Mr. Chong's apartment."

"Did you know those men?"

"They are evil men. They work for...er I think you call them the Mafia."

"Mafia! Are you sure? They didn't look at all Italian."

"Oh, no, sir, they are from Hong Kong."

"You mean the Chinese Mafia?"

"Yes."

"What do they want with Mr. Chong?"

"I don't know, sir. They had been watching Mr. Chong's place for a week now. Waiting for him to come home."

"Do you know Mr. Chong?"

"Yes, he's a friend of mine. He disappeared five days ago."

This case was beginning to get me down. Everybody was disappearing on me.

"Did he tell you where he was going?"

"No, just that he had to get away from here. Are you a friend of his?"

"Yes, I am a friend. Look, I appreciate you coming and telling me this, but there isn't much I can do about that."

"I know, I just thought that if you run into him, you'll tell him Mia Ling was asking about him."

She turned and walked out the door. I asked her if there was anything she needed before she left. She seemed like a powerful woman; she said no and left. I just wanted to get a good night's sleep and think about it in the morning. Besides, I wanted to take one last look for Mr. Chong before I left.

When I awoke, it was nine a.m. I got up and took a shower and went downstairs to the dining room for breakfast. While eating breakfast, I started thinking about the first time I came out to San Francisco. I was eighteen years old, and I was on my way to Japan. The Air Force was going to fly us over in one of their transports. I was so excited when I arrived that I went for a walk. I remember turning the corner, and when I saw that the street went almost straight uphill, I turned around and went back to my hotel room. I had to be at Travis Air Force Base the next day. I didn't feel like tackling the hill. I started laughing to myself as I thought about how young I was.

The next morning, I ate breakfast. I checked out of the Motel and stopped off at Chinatown on my way to the airport. This time I went to the Asian cleaners next door to Mr. Chong's apartment. There was a young girl behind the counter. At first, she didn't want to talk to me. I convinced her I wouldn't hurt her and that all I wanted is some information about Mr. Chong.

"I don't know what you want me to say, sir."

"Well, did you know Mr. Chong?"

"The man next door only came in here to get his clothes once a week. He never talked much. Except, the last time he was here."

"What did he say?"

"Just that he had a little girl like me a long time ago. She lives east somewhere, and he was going to visit her."

"When was that?"

"About four or five days ago."

"Did anyone ask about Mr. Chong?"

"Yes, two days ago, two men came in and asked about Mr. Chong. They looked like they were with the Hei Shou Tang. I told them the same thing I told you."

"What is the Hei Shou Tang?

"It's what you call...ah...The Black Hand gang."

"You mean the Chinese Mafia?"

"Yes, that's what you call it."

"Thank you."

As I walked outside, I got this eerie feeling in the pit of my stomach. If Mr. Chong was heading to New York to see his daughter and the two men that beat on me yesterday found the information in Mr. Chong's apartment after they finished with me. They might be following him to New York. So, what the hell am I doing standing here in the middle of Chinatown in San Francisco? I found a telephone and called the number Michael gave me. I told him I was on my way to the airport and he was to meet me as soon as possible.

On my way to the airport, one thing kept bothering me about this whole thing. If Maggie didn't find her father and her father didn't know she was missing. Who the hell was holding the girl, and why? This case was getting more and more complicated. When I got to the airport, Michael was waiting for me. We took off immediately. The weather was clear with a fifteen mile an hour tailwind. That was good that would put us in New York at about six-thirty p.m. I called Michael up-front and told him to put a call through to Vera and to express her to have Maxine pick me up at the airport. There wasn't much I could do until then but sit back and wait. I tried to get some sleep that always passes the time quicker.

CHAPTER FIVE

When we arrived at Linden Airport, it was about five-forty. Maxine was there right on time I told her to take me to Alex's place.

When we got their Suzy was downstairs in the restaurant as usual. I went upstairs and knocked on Alex's door. When he opened it, he looked like he had been on a three-day binge. I tried to sober him up with coffee. It was no use. I took him back to my place for a night of good night's sleep and where I could keep an eye on him. I wanted to ask him some questions in the morning when he was comfortable and sober. When I got to the apartment, I put him to sleep in the spare room. I took a shower and went to bed myself.

Alex awakened me; he was asking me how he got here. I had to calm him down first.

"Alex, Alex, will you stop that shouting? If you calm down, I'll explain how you got here."

"Okay, I'm calm. Now how the hell did I get here?"

I climbed out of bed and put on my bathrobe and went into the kitchen to get some coffee. I asked Alex if he wanted some.

"No, dammit. I want to know what the hell I'm doing in your apartment."

"I brought you here from your apartment. Yesterday when I got back into town, I stopped by your place to talk to you. You were in no condition to speak. So

I brought you back here to get a good night's sleep. You looked like you needed it."

"Yeah, well, I was a little under the weather."

"You want to tell me why you started drinking. You never drank in Nam."

"That's a long story."

"I've got time."

"I'll have some of that coffee."

I poured him a cup of coffee, and we sat at the kitchen table, and he began to tell me the story.

"Well, it all started after you left to go back to the states back in Feb. of '76. It was just after the big Exodus out of Saigon. You had been gone for about six weeks when I got my discharge orders back in Mar. of '76. The C.O. was getting on my case about taking Maggie back to the States with me. You know the story, how the family wouldn't accept her, and the American people, in general, would resent her. He had been on my case for a couple of weeks now, and my patience was wearing thin. I got mad and ran out of the office, hopped in a jeep, and drove off the base to cool off. I went into the first bar I came to and had a drink. I guess I thought it wouldn't hurt anything. I was wrong; one drink led to another and another until finally, I was drunk. Next thing I remember, I woke up in the Army Hospital with Maggie by my side, the C.O. looking down at me, he was saying something about my having an accident while running over a little Vietnamese girl named Kim Ho, she was only nine years old. He didn't know whether the family was going to press charges or not.

Later I found out the little girl had no parents, and she was disabled for life. She would have trouble walking for a long time. I guess I went crazy. I tried to see her when I got out of the hospital, but she had disappeared. You know how Saigon was at that time, chaotic and all. She transferred to a civilian hospital. After that, they didn't know where she had gone. No charges were pending against me, and finally, I got discharged, and Maggie and I went back to the States. I had the Red Cross searching for her for two months after I got back, but they couldn't find her. After that, I couldn't get her out of my mind. I kept having this same nightmare with a little Vietnamese girl in a wheelchair. She had no face, and she kept repeating over and over, 'it's your fault, it's your fault.' Then I'd wake up in a cold sweat."

"Didn't the Red Cross ever locate her."

"No, I started drinking a lot to try to forget. It didn't work. Things got worse; I couldn't hold a job because of my drinking. I don't know how Maggie stayed with me this long. She had to get a job so we could get by. Things were getting better before she disappeared."

"What about the dream?"

"I still have it from time to time but not as often. I guess I'm thinking of Maggie when I'm not having the dream. I can't sleep nights unless I drink myself to sleep."

"I'll make a deal with you; you straighten yourself out and stop the drinking, and I'll look for Maggie, and at the same time, I'll have my secretary consider this little girl's disappearance. Do you have a picture of her or anything?"

"No, all I know about her is her name is Kim Ho, and she was nine years old at the time."

"Well, that would make her about thirteen or fourteen years old now. I'll have Vera check it out, and we'll see."

"Thanks, Brent, I don't know what to say."

"Don't say anything. Just go home and get your shit together."

After Alex left, I started thinking. This case didn't seem like it was getting any closer to getting solved than it did ten days ago. I didn't find out much in San Francisco. I mean the city may be pretty, romantic and people may want to leave their hearts there. I almost left my whole body there, and it wouldn't have been by choice.

It was about noon; I decided to get dressed and go down to the office. First,

I called and told Vera to check with the Red Cross and the Vietnamese Embassy. I wanted to see what she could find out about a car accident involving a Sgt. Lomax's and a nine-year-old girl back in Mar. of 1976 in Saigon. I also told her to try to set up a meeting with Mama Castellano. I had a few questions for her and also get Bill Singer on the phone.

After my shower, I got dressed and went downstairs. I walked into the office and greeted Vera with the usual smile. Then I walked into my office and waited for Vera to get Bill on the phone. After a few minutes, Vera got on the intercom and told me she had Bill on the line.

"Hello, Bill, how are you doing?"

"Brent, I've been trying to reach you, but Vera said you were out of town."

"Yes, I went to San Francisco to see if I could find Maggie's father."

"Well, did you?"

"No. All I got for my troubles was to get beat up and left in an alley in Chinatown."

"Yeah, well, that figures. Listen, I just found out you had a visitor a couple of days ago. Mama Castellano no less, why didn't you tell me?"

"I didn't think it was important."

"Important, anytime Mama Castellano makes an appearance, more so if it's in a Private Investigators office. What did she want, anyway?"

"You know I can't tell you that. That's privileged information."

"Oh, c' mon, you're not going to pull that routine on me, are you?"

"Look, Bill; it's all speculative right now. I don't want to involve anyone, especially

Mama Castellano if there's no truth to it. Right now, I can't prove anything, and I don't know anything yet. I promise as soon as I find out something, I'll let you know. Honest."

"Okay, Brent. Just remember I'm watching you, and if you're out of line, I'll pull your license. Remember that."

"You're such a pal. It's reassuring to know I have a guardian angel watching over me. 'Your one in a million Bill.'

"Yeah, sure. Goodbye."

I hung up the phone and walked out to Vera's desk.

"Did you get a hold of Mama Castellano yet?"

"No, but I did get a hold of Jack Todd. He said he would set up a meeting with her in his office at three this afternoon."

Good, that will give me time to get a bite at Sardie's. Have Maxine pick me up downstairs in five minutes."

"I already called and told her to meet you downstairs."

"Thanks, Vera, you're one in a million."

While driving over to Sardie's, I saw a car pull up alongside us. Before I knew what happened, and an Asian gentleman pulled out a pistol with a silencer on it. He fired three shots at my window and drove off down the street. I told Maxine to follow them, but she lost them in the traffic. I'm glad I took Maxine's advice when we bought this car and got bulletproof windows. Maxine said she would be able to get the license plate number. I told her to drop me off and get in touch with Vera and have her check it out. As I entered Sardie's, George, the steward, showed me to my usual table.

"Hello, Mr. Stewart, how are you doing today?"

"Fine, George. What's the special today?"

"Shrimp cocktail to start, followed by Swordfish a la Fresca."

"Sounds good. I'll have one. Oh, and I'll have a screwdriver while I'm waiting."

"Excellent, sir."

I'd been coming here ever since I hit the lottery. I like eating where the stars dine. They're such showmen even when they're eating. Everything is more significant than life to them. I often wonder what they do when they're alone. While I was thinking about it, Ms. Lola Fontaine walked by, waved at me, and said hi. Lola had been the toast of this town for as long as I could remember. Every time you turn around, you see her name on a billboard someplace in town. She prefers doing a play to going to a movie in Hollywood. She says the people in Hollywood are not real. They have no heart. They're all business. They are out to get whatever they can out of you. The agents are the worst. Most of them don't care what kind of work they get you so long as they get their ten percent. Oh well, I guess that's show biz. About then, George brought me my drink. I was about to take a sip when I heard this deep voice.

"Well, if it isn't Brent baby. The only P.I. in New York that doesn't have to work."

I turned and saw Pete Ryan. The man that writes everything he sees at Sardie's in his column. He's the show business's answer to Walter Cronkite. Anybody in town that is anybody ends up in his column at some point in time. I have, on occasion, myself much to my dismay.

"Well, Pete, won't you join me for a drink?"

Pete sat down and ordered a drink from the waiter.

"Tell me, Brent, what are you working on now. The murder of some agent by their client?"

I don't like to say too much to Pete. You never know what's going to end up in his column.

"No, Pete. I'm just having a quiet lunch."

"Say, when are you going to let me do a piece on your Chauffeur?"

"Maxine? You know there's no story there. Maxine is just working for me to help support her poor old grandmother."

"Sure, I believe you. I want to hear Maxine say that. Seriously Brent, do you have anything for me?"

"Nothing you would be interested in Pete."

"Well, I'd better get out of here before you ruin my reputation. People see me with you; they might think I'm having trouble with my wife."

"Your one in a million, Pete."

As Pete was leaving, the waiter was bringing my dinner over, it looked great, and I told him so.

By the time Maxine got back to me, I had just finished eating. She was pulling up as I walked outside. I climbed in told her to take me to Todd's office. On the way, I asked her if she found out anything about the sharpshooter that re-designed my window.

"Yes, Mr. Stewart, the car was leased to two gentlemen from San Francisco.

According to the leasing agent, they got off the plane yesterday."

"Hmmm. That means if the two gentlemen are tracking Mr. Chong, he must be in town somewhere. He'll probably try to contact Alex or Maggie. I tell Vera when I get to the office."

The case was developing into an interesting one. If I were a writer, I'd write a story about it, oh well. We arrived at the office I up and told Vera to call Mr. Lomax on the phone, and I went into my office.

"I have Mr. Lomax on the phone, Mr. Stewart."

"Hello, Alex, listen. I have reason to believe that Mr. Chong may try to contact you. If he does, hold him there until I get there, okay?"

"Brent, he already called me. I told him about Maggie missing. He took it pretty hard; Mr. Chong said he was coming over tonight and that he had something to tell me."

"I have a meeting to go to right now. I'll come over after my meeting. I have a few questions for Mr. Chong. Keep him there for me."

"You got it; I'll see you later, Brent."

Later, Maxine pulled up in front of Mr. Todd's office for our meeting. I got out and told Maxine to wait for me.

I walked inside; Mrs. Scotto looked up and smiled. I told Mrs. Scotto; I had an appointment.

"Yes, Mr. Stewart, go right on in."

When I entered the office, I wasn't expecting the whole Castellano family there. Jack Todd was sitting behind the desk. Mama Castellano was sitting on the sofa with her other two sons Michael and Sonny, by her side. I walked in and sat down. Jack was the first to speak.

"Well, Mr. Stewart, what can we do for you?"

"I wanted to talk to Mrs. Castellano."

"She's listening; go ahead."

"Okay. In trying to locate Mrs. Lomax, I went out to San Francisco to locate her father, to see if he knew anything about his daughter. While I was there, I had a run-in with two men from the 'Hei Shou Tang' or the Black Hand gang. They made it clear that they, too, were looking for Mr. Chong. I was not able to find him while I was out there. I spoke to a friend of his who said these two men had been watching his place. I was hoping you might be able to enlighten me on the nature of their business with Mr. Chong."

Jack looked at Mama Castellano, and she looked back at him without saying anything, just the slightest nod of her head.

Jack spoke, "Well, Mr. Stewart, the two men you mentioned are not from our family. As you well know, there are families like ours all over the world. Just as business deals are going on around the world, Mr. Chong may be involved with his own private business. We are not aware of what it is."

Just then, Sonny jumped in and said, "If we were, we wouldn't tell no private dick what it was, that's for sure."

Jack spoke, "Sonny be quiet; I'll handle this. Mr. Stewart, you'll have to excuse my younger brother; he has a lot to learn."

"I got that impression. Don't worry, and I don't want to involve the family in this. If they have nothing to do with this as you say, then there's no need. I want your cooperation in this matter."

"How can we help you?"

"Maybe you can find out what Mr. Chong's business is with those two men. It might have some bearing as to why Maggie is missing."

The whole time I sat, their Mama said nothing. It was is evident that Jack was speaking for the family, for the time being anyway. Mama just sat there and observed everything.

Jack spoke again, "We'll find out what we can. We want to cooperate in helping to find Maggie. Everybody likes Maggie in the office. Now if you will excuse us, Mr. Stewart, we do have a business to run.

We'll contact you as soon as we find out anything."

I got up and went to the door. "Thank you, Mrs. Castellano. I appreciate your help in this matter."

As I walked to the car, I wondered just how much they knew and weren't telling me. I told Maxine to drive me to Alex's apartment in Chinatown.

Maxine pulled up in front of the Choy Inn as it started to rain. Spring rain in New York is like no other. When it's over, you feel as though your troubles are gone away.

I told Maxine to wait as I went inside. Suzy was at the bar getting ready for the evening dinner crowd. "I'll see you in a minute," I said.

I went on upstairs to Alex's apartment. When I knocked, Alex answered and told me to come in. He looked nervously down the hall behind me. As I walked inside, this middle-aged Chinese man was sitting on the couch.

"Brent, I want you to meet Mr. Chong, Maggie's father. Mr. Chong, I would like you to meet an old friend of mine, Mr. Stewart."

"How are you, Mr. Chong? It's nice to meet you."

Mr. Chong stood up and bowed as he said, "Hello."

He looked to be about sixty-three or so. He stood at about five-foot-three.

"Mr. Chong, when was the last time you saw Maggie?"

"About... a year ago, she came out for a visit."

"Why did you want Maggie to visit you this time?"

He looked at me but didn't say anything. It was as though he didn't want to.

"Mr. Chong, I'm trying to help you and your daughter. If you know anything that will help, tell me now."

"About two weeks ago, I received a visit from two men."

"Do they work for the 'Hei Shou Tang'?"

When I said that, his face turned white, and he sat back on the couch and looked at me for a minute.

"How did you know about the 'Hei Shou Tang'?"

"Never mind. That's not important right now. Go on."

"They wanted what I took from them."

"What was that?"

"Uncut diamonds, two million dollars' worth."

Alex looked at me in amazement. I must say I was a little taken back by it also. I looked at the older man again. He just sat there very calmly and looked at us with a smile.

"How did you get your hands on two million dollars' worth of diamonds?"

"It was straightforward, Mr. Stewart. About ten years ago, just after Alex here married my Maggie and came back to the states. I moved to Hong Kong; as you know, Vietnam was getting a little hot."

"I seem to recall we had a pot boiling in the Far East around that time. Go on."

"I got a job working for an import-export company there. I found out later that it belonged to the Hei Shou Tang. The job they had me doing at the time gave me easy access to their revenue. It was around that time I also made friends with a couple of diplomats working at the American Embassy as couriers. They would come into the shop and buy some Chinese artifacts."

"What's all this got to do with your daughter?"

"I'm coming to that, patience, my American friend."

"I must say, you're doing it the long way around."

"Hold up, Alex. Let's hear the old man out. Go ahead, Mr. Chong."

"Thank you. I'm sure you know couriers coming into this country have Diplomatic immunity. They don't search for Diplomatic workers when they enter. I made a deal with them if they would help me smuggle the diamonds into this country. I would give them each a third. Unfortunately, one of them got killed before he could leave Hong Kong. The Hei Shou Tang are not too forgiving when they find a traitorous member."

"What did you do with the diamonds when you got them into the country?"

"You'll like this part. When my friend from the American embassy brought the diamonds to me, I had to find a safe place for them, someplace where nobody would think to look. I have this old coat I brought with me from Viet Nam. So, I sewed the diamonds in the lining of the coat. I have it on now. I'm never without it."

As he said, he had this great big grin on his face. I will say one thing about the old guy. He's clever.

"What about your friend from the Embassy, did you give him his share?"

"Well, I was going to...but; it slipped my mind on purpose."

"Mr. Chong, did Alex tell you about your daughter missing?"

"Brent, I was just telling him that when you arrived."

"Have you any idea where she might have gone, Mr. Chong?"

"No, I don't. When I found out those men were looking for me in San Francisco. I figured I'd better leave town. I sent that letter to Maggie telling her to come to San Francisco so I could tell her everything about the diamonds. When she didn't show up, I decided to come here."

"What is the name of your friend in the American Embassy in Hong Kong?"

"I'm afraid you won't find him there."

"When I didn't show up with his share of the diamonds at the place we had prearranged. I called him a couple of days later at the Embassy office in San Francisco. They told me he had disappeared."

"What was his name? I'll check it out and see if we can locate him."

"His name is Matthew Simms, but it won't do any good."

"Mr. Chong. It's safe to assume that those two men who beat on me in San Francisco are the same men that were on your tail. They don't have your daughter. The only person that would have any reason to take your daughter would be Matthew Simms. He's probably keeping her in a safe place to trade her later for the diamonds. We have to find her before those two men locate you."

"How are we going to find her?"

"I don't think we'll have to. If my guess is right, Simms will find us. All we have to do is sit tight."

"Brent, what's our next move?"

"First thing, we'll have to get a safe place for Mr. Chong. I know just the place."

"I know this sweet lady in Brooklyn that loves company. Mr. Chong can stay there. You keep him here until I arrange things there. I'll get back to you."

As I left the apartment and headed downstairs, I was thinking how mother was going to enjoy this.

Chapter Six

My mother had lived alone since my father died back in 1966. When I parlayed my money in the stock market, I bought her a townhouse on shore road in Brooklyn. She's sixty-five and a "Woman of the World." She has a live-in maid that's more like a roommate. My mother is from Virginia, and she's my stepmother. She makes liars out of all those stories we used to hear about stepmothers when I was growing up in Brooklyn with my sister. She's the most loving mother I've ever seen. She raised my sister and me; she did a great job. I mean, look at us. My sister is married to a successful businessman. He owns his own company and did a great job of taking care of his family. She lives in this beautiful home in Staten Island and plays golf with her husband all over the world. She has five grown children two, of which are married.

I didn't turn out so bad either, and I don't have a wife and kids yet, but, in my business, it's hard to get started on one. Anyway, getting back to my mother, she always likes a little adventure in her life. I think she'll enjoy the intrigue. I'll stop by in the morning to see her.

As I re-entered the restaurant, I could see those two men from San Francisco talking to Suzy. They didn't see me yet. I turned around and ran back upstairs. It looks like Mother is going to get an early visit. I figured they weren't here to shake Alex's hand. I got back up to Alex's apartment and asked Alex if there was a back exit in this place.

"No, but we can use this fire-escape."

"Let's go; we don't have much time."

I helped Mr. Chong out of the window. Alex went first; I went last and closed the window. We got downstairs and around the front to where Maxine was waiting in the car. After Mr. Chong got in the car with Alex, I told Maxine to get them out of here. Before she could get in the car, the two men came out of the front and saw us. They came over and grabbed Maxine to push her out of the way. She threw a sidekick on the first one's face that sent him crashing to the ground before he knew what hit him. The second one drew his gun. Before he could use it, she caught his gun hand with another kick. Then hit him in the face with her hand that sent him down fast.

"Get in the car, Mr. Stewart."

She didn't have to tell me twice. As I climbed in, she ran around to the other side and got in and drove off. As we drove away, I could see two very large Asians lying on the street. I'm sure when they come to, they will think twice before they tangle with Maxine again. This was not the first time Maxine has helped me out of a tight jam. Of course, that's why I hired her. I told Maxine to make for my mothers' house in Brooklyn.

On the way over there, I explained to Mr. Chong that he would be staying at my Mother's house for a while, and for his safety, it would be best he didn't tell anyone where he was staying.

When we arrived in front of my mothers' townhouse, she was out front, watering the little garden she had planted. Mom loved to relax by working on her shrubbery. She greeted me with her usual motherly attitude.

"Well, you know I have a son that looks just like you. Maybe you've seen him. He likes to play detective."

"C' mon Mom, I'm sorry I didn't make it over on Thursday, but I've been working hard on this case."

"Who is this. My new housekeeper?"

"No, Mom, this is Mr. Chong, and he needs a place to stay."

"You want to hide him, you mean."

"Okay, have it your way, mom. I'm looking for his daughter, and two goons are after him. Here is the only place I could bring him."

"Don't just stand out here. Come on inside, and I don't want my flowers ruined with your falling bodies when the shooting starts."

I always did like moms' dry wit. She lost it for a long time after Dad died. Now she's getting back on track. She took us into the kitchen and made us some coffee.

"Have you at least called your sister in a while?"

"Yes, I spoke to her last week. She told me to be sure to show up for Laura's wedding next month or don't show up at all. You know Caryl. She and Bill are going to have their hands filled with this Wedding. Of course, it won't be as hectic as Susan's was. They are getting the hang of it now. By the time, the youngest one is ready to get married, Bill will give her husband-to-be, a nice strong ladder so they can flee."

"Bills been asking where you were, he said he contacted the office a few times to see if you wanted to play some golf. You never returned his calls."

"Yes, I know, mom, as I told you before, I'm working on a crucial case."

"So, tell me about this important case you're on."

"I can't."

"What, are you a big shot now? You can't tell your mother."

"It's not that; it's just that the less you know, the safer it is for you. I don't want you in any danger."

"What danger?"

"Mother, will you stop talking like a Jewish mother and be your old lovable self. The caring, loving Irish mother, I've grown to love."

"Okay, you just be careful, and call me every day."

"I will mom, now make Mr. Chong comfortable, and I'll get back to you. Mr. Chong, my mother, will show you to your room. I'll let you know the minute I hear anything about your daughter."

"Mrs. Stewart, I hope I'm not putting you out."

"Of course, not Mr. Chong. It's a pleasure to have your company. Mr. Chong, have you ever had corn beef and cabbage?"

"No, Mrs. Stewart. Have you ever eaten shark fin soup?"

I left the house, climbed into the car. I had a feeling that the two of them would enjoy each other's company.

Chapter Seven

I told Maxine to stop by Sammy's old newsstand before we headed back to the city. I wanted to check on Laura to see if she needed anything. When we got there, she was getting ready to close.

"Hi, Laura. How have you been?"

"Okay, I have a buyer for the newsstand."

"That's great. Are you hungry? How would you like to get a bite to eat?"

"Sounds great. Give me a couple of minutes to close."

I told Maxine to call it a night and that I would see her tomorrow. When I went back to the newsstand, Laura was ready to go.

"Well, where would you like to eat?"

"You like Italian food? I know this nice place about a block from here."

"Why are we waiting? Let's go."

As we walked to the restaurant, we talked. I learned one thing; Laura is much younger than I thought. She likes older men because she says, "They know how to treat women." I could also tell by talking to her that she ran in the fast lanes at school. She liked to smoke pot, although she wasn't into the heavy stuff like acid and heroin.

When we got to the restaurant, the waiter seated us by a window, and it had just started to rain outside. We ordered a drink and talked some more.

"So, tell me, Brent, why didn't you ever marry?"

"I guess I haven't met the right women yet."

"Maybe you're not looking in the right places!"

"That may be true. In my line of work, you don't meet available women. I mean, they are either in trouble with their husbands or boyfriends. I don't need that kind of woman."

"What kind do you need?"

"Well, I guess you could say I'm looking for a free spirit. Someone that's not tied down to one person and doesn't want to be. One without so much baggage of her own that she forgets a man is a person, with needs and desires."

"Exciting Brent. You don't just have the money you have brains too. You know you're not a bad-looking man. The first time I met you, I thought you were one of those hard-nosed detective types. Underneath that hard shell ticks a heart."

As she talked, she put her hand on mine and smiled. I got the distinct impression she was setting me up for something. When I first saw her, I thought she was beautiful. Now that I've had time to chat and get to know her a little more, I'm finding out. There's something mysterious about her too. Something I can't quite figure out yet.

"So, tell me, are you planning to stay in the city long?"

She looked at me and smiled slyly and said, "Why, do you have plans for me?"

"Well, I wouldn't put it quite that way, but I guess you could say that if you wanted to."

"Sounds interesting."

Just then, the waiter came and took our order. There wasn't much talking after that.

I guess we both were doing some head-trips on each other with our eyes. After we finished eating, I asked her if she would like to go inside to the bar and get a drink.

"Sure, why not. I'd love to."

"Tell me, Ms. Wilson..."

"Laura."

"Yes...er Laura, so tell me about this buyer for the Newsstand. Have you met him yet?"

"I did. I'm supposed to see Mr. Jones again tomorrow, and then it's back to school for me."

While we were talking, I spotted my two friends on the other side of the room, staring at us. They saw me looking at them and nodded their heads and smiled. I had this knotted-feeling in the pit of my stomach.

"Look, Laura, I want you to do just what I tell you to do, no questions asked, and I'll explain it tomorrow. Okay?"

"Sure, but what's going on?"

"Laura, two men have been tailing me. I can't explain it now, but if they see me yelling at you, they'll think we're not very good friends. Slap me."

"What?"

"Slap me and leave. Make it look good, and I'll call you tomorrow."

Laura stood up, looked at me and slapped me on the face, and said, "I will do no such thing you...you...pervert." Then she left. I sat there for a moment. I wondered if she took drama lessons at that college she was going to. She had me convinced that I said something out of line. As she walked out, I looked around the room, and people were looking at me. So were my two friends. I downed my drink and got up and left.

When I got outside, the street was empty. It was close to eleven p.m. Of course, and there were no taxis. There never is one in this town when you want one. I started walking toward the subway. The two men came out of the bar and followed me. I started walking faster, trying to lose them. There was a subway entrance on the corner. I figured that if I could get to the subway, I'd be all right. I made my way downstairs and went to the booth to get a token. There was an older man in the box.

"Evening' mister. How's your night?

"Fine. Let me have a couple of tokens."

As I headed toward the turnstile, I saw my two friends hot on my tail. I went through and headed to the Manhattan side of the tracks and went down the stairs. When I got to the bottom, luck was with me. The train was pulling in. I figured those guys would be right behind me. I hid behind one of those posts and watched the stairs. Sure, enough they came running down the stairs and jumped on the train just as the train doors were closing. I stood there smiling and waving as the train pulled out of the station, they didn't look so happy. They were shaking their fist at me as they rode away. I went to a phone booth and called Alex.

"Brent, I'm glad you called. Simms just contacted me. He wants to meet with me tomorrow morning at Nathan's restaurant on Broadway at ten o'clock. What'll I do?"

"Meet Simms, of course. I'll be there too. Alex don't worry about a thing. Everything is going to be all right. I'll see you in the morning."

"He said if I brought anyone else, I wouldn't see Maggie again."

"Don't worry. Simms won't see me, neither will you, but I'll be there. Good-night."

I headed back to my apartment. It was going to be an exciting day tomorrow. I wanted to get some shut-eye and be ready for it. First, I wanted to make a couple of phone calls when I got back.

I walked into the lobby of my apartment; Johnny was standing there with a big smile. Like always.

"Evening, Johnny, how's it going?"

"Evening' Mr. Stewart, fine sir. My little boy had a fight with some kid at school today, and the kid knocked his braces out. Now I've got to go back to the dentist and have them put back in. My boy isn't too happy about that. You know how boys are."

"Yeah, boys will be boys. Good-night, Johnny."

I made my way to the elevator and went in. As the doors closed, I kept thinking about those two guys. I must keep the two guys off my back until I get Maggie back. I know just who can help me out. The elevator reached my floor, and I got out. I took out Mr. Todd's phone number. The one he gave me to use if I needed him for anything. Boy, did I need him? He answered after the second ring.

"Mr. Todd, this is Brent Stewart. I need your help."

I could tell by his reply; he was happy to hear that. People in his line of business like to do favors, that way, other people owe them favors, and they love to collect them. I was hoping he wouldn't ask why I wanted this favor.

"I need you to take the heat off me with two of the Chinese families' goons. Long enough to find out what they wanted."

He said he would, but he wanted all the answers in two days or else. Two days wasn't much, but I didn't have too many choices. I agreed and hung up. He said he would get back to me later. Next, I called Maxine and told her I had a little job I wanted her to do for me. I figured I'd have Maxine watch Mr. Simms just in case I lost him tomorrow. After I spoke to Maxine, I took a nice hot shower and hit the sack. I was exhausted.

I arrived at Nathan's about nine-thirty. It's not the best time of the day to have their famous hot dogs, but what the hell. I haven't followed a strict diet since I got out of the service. I ordered one hot dog and an orange drink, not to mention the famous Nathan's

French fries. Every time I eat at Nathan's, it reminds me of the original Nathan's in Coney Island. I used to go there all the time as a kid. Coney Island was a fun place we had the Cyclone, the Parachute ride, and who could forget the Steeple Chase rides. Afterward, we would walk on the boardwalk and look at all the cute girls on the beach. When you finished a day at Coney Island, you were exhausted, ready for the long ride back on the subway to Brooklyn. The one ride I hated as a kid was the Wonder Wheel. It was huge, and the seats are enclosed in a cage that pivoted on a track to swing you out then back. It scared the shit out of me.

I remember I went on with my mother when I was small. The wheel went around once, and I cried all the way around. My mother told the man to stop the wheel after one turn. I never went on that sucker again.

As I was eating my hot dog, I saw Alex coming in and walking up to this man to talk to him. I couldn't tell what they were saying but the man he was talking to looked mad. After about five minutes, the man left. I followed him outside and saw Maxine across the street. I gave her the hi sign. I pointed it to the man to follow. She was on him like a hooker on payday. I went back inside to talk to Alex.

"Well, Alex, what did the cheerful bastard have to say?"

"He said he has Maggie and showed me her wedding ring. It was hers. I remember I bought it for her when we hit New York just after we arrived from Saigon. He said he wanted his share of the Diamonds, or Maggie would die. He said he would call to tell me when and where the drop would be. I told him if Maggie was hurt in any way. He gave me this tape; he said I could play it when I got home."

Alex showed me a cassette tape Mr. Simms had given him.

"Okay, let's go home and wait for Maxine to show."

I didn't say anything to Alex, but I was hoping that Maxine was okay and didn't lose him. Right now, she was the only lead we had to find Maggie.

We went back to my office to wait to hear from Maxine. I stopped off in Brooklyn to pick up Mr. Chong. If anything came up, I wanted Mr. Chong to be right there. When we got to the office, Mr. Todd had called and left a message. He said, 'Those two gentlemen are now on leashes, and I had thirty-six hours left. Time was running out.

After about an hour, I was starting to get a little worried. Then the phone rang, and it was Maxine. She said she was on her way back and would explain everything when she got there. Alex was starting to get edgy and pacing back and forth. I could tell by the look on his face that he wanted a drink bad. Mr. Chong, on the other hand, was your typical Asian. He sat there in my office without an emotion showing on his face. Those Asian eyes are staring into space like a beacon in the night.

Maxine came bursting in the front door, all out of breath and trying to talk.

"Mr. Stewart, I followed them just like you wanted me to. They drove over to Jersey. To a town just off route forty-six, on Church Street in Lodi."

"Did they see you?"

"No, I don't think so. Mr. Stewart, I saw Maggie, or at least I think it was her.

She looked like the picture you showed me, but..."

"Continue."

"Well..."

She looked at Alex and then to Mr. Chong and then back to me. She looked as though she didn't want to say what she saw.

"Well, I was looking through the window of this house, and I saw this woman that looked like Maggie. She was smiling at the two men. I couldn't tell what they were saying. It didn't appear to me as though she was being held there against her will."

"Are you saying my wife is in with these men against her father?"

"No, I just think that maybe we were made to believe one thing when it's something else."

"That's ridiculous. I won't stand here and listen to all this shit. Brent, I thought you were on my side."

"Alex, now calm down. I am on your side. Let's not jump to any hasty conclusions before we find out all the details. Mr. Chong, you haven't said much through all this."

"I only know that the children may not always turn out the way the parents would like them to. Still, no matter how they turn out, the parents will always love them. That is the way of life."

Mr. Chong was beginning to sound like a fortune cookie. I told Alex to put on the tape to see if we could get any clues from that. As he played it, I watched the look on his face. I could tell it was tearing him up inside. Hearing her voice, not knowing how much danger she was in, I'm sure what

Maxine said didn't help any either. As I listened to Maggie's speech on the tape, I tried to picture her with that beautiful face. She didn't say much except that Mr. Chong should give them what they wanted. Also, that she was all right for now, but she's scared and wants to come home. She referred to Alex as honey. That got me thinking about what Alex had said about them not using those kinds of phrases to each other. She seems to be trying to warn Alex about something. Something didn't feel right, but I couldn't put my finger on it.

"Look, Alex, you and Mr. Chong go back to your apartment and wait for Mr. Simms to call you. Maxine and I have an errand to run."

"Okay, Brent, but let me know the minute you find out anything about Maggie."

As Mr. Chong and Alex left the office and headed back to the apartment, I turned to Maxine.

"Look, Maxine; you're going to take me back to that house in Lodi. We are going to get to the bottom of this right now."

"Ah c' mon Mr. Stewart, I need some rest. Can't we go first thing in the morning?"

"Okay, go on home and get some sleep, but be at my place in the morning at five o'clock, understand?"

"Five O'clock. How come so early?"

"I want us to get out there before they get up. Maybe we can take them by surprise."

"All right, I'll see you in the morning."

I sat there in my office with the lights out after Maxine had gone home. I was trying to figure out this case. I was hoping for Alex's sake that Maxine's hunch about Maggie wasn't exact. It would kill Alex for sure. I'm sure Alex was no jewel to live with these past ten years. Well, I wasn't going to think about it anymore tonight.

I made my way to the elevator and pushed the button. When the door opened, there stood Suzy looking at her sexy self. She pulled me into the elevator and pushed the penthouse button. As the door closed, Suzy put her arms around me. They pulled me close to her and gave me one of those kisses that said, "No more business tonight, sweetheart."

As the elevator door opened at my apartment, Suzy already had her dress off. She draped the dress over her shoulder. Suzy didn't wear a bra. She just stood there in her panties, looking like the most desirable woman in the world.

"The boss let me have the rest of the night off. I thought you might want some company, was I wrong?"

"Are you kidding? You make it hard for a guy to say no."

"That's the idea."

We made our way into the bedroom. She sat me down on the edge of the bed and began to undress me, starting with my shoes. I sat there looking down at her beautiful face, thinking this is how life was meant to be. Having someone that cares about you and makes you feel good at the end of a hard day's work. By the time she got me down to my shorts, she was kissing me all over my body. I was ready to explode, and she knew it.

"Relax, Brent; I want this to last."

She was enjoying it as much as I was, and that's what made it so respectable. I could hear a police siren going off down the street somewhere. I didn't care; I was here for the night.

Chapter Eight

The morning sun came through my window and gently woke me. When I looked, Suzy was gone. She left a note on my pillow.

"Have to run, love you. Call me later."

I got up and took a shower. While I was getting dressed, the buzzer from downstairs rang. When I answered it, it was Maxine. I told her I would be right down.

As we headed up the West Side Highway toward the George Washington Bridge, I could see all the people driving to work. People always look like they are in a daze in the morning. Maybe it's because they've just awakened. You see, cars go by with women driving while putting on their make-up. It always amazed me how they don't have more accidents. The men are drinking their morning coffee and smoking the fourth or fifth cigarette. The traffic was starting to build up as we approached the bridge. I love the overpasses in this city. They seem to tell a story. They are like the hands of people, holding the metropolis together and bringing them closer.

As we headed down Main Street in Lodi, we passed under an overpass of Route 46. Next to the exit ramp was a restaurant called 'Casa Siros.' I remember I used to go to that place years ago. I knew the owners. They had a sexy daughter whose name was Rosalie. She wasn't just sensual; she had a head-on her shoulders and was charming to speak to at any time. She always knew the right thing to say. Anyway, we headed down Main Street to Church and made a left. We parked the car on the corner and walked to the house. I didn't want to alert anyone we were coming.

When we got to the house, I told Maxine to cover the back door, and I would go in the front. I went to the front door and knocked. I didn't expect anyone to answer. Was I surprised when a sweet looking old lady answered the door!

"Yes, can I help you?"

"Are you the lady of the house?"

"Yes, what do you want?"

"I'm sorry; I was looking for a much younger woman?"

"You should have stopped here about twenty years ago. I was younger than."

"I mean...I was looking for a young Chinese woman."

"You'll have to go to Chinatown for that, I'm afraid."

"Do you live alone?"

"Yes, unless you got plans, and if you do forget them. I don't go out with younger men."

This lady was confusing me.

"Look, lady; I'm looking for an Asian woman in her middle to late twenties and two gentlemen. I was told they live here."

"Well, you're welcome to come in and look, but I can assure you I'm the only one here. I've lived here alone since my husband died back in '69."

It was about that time that Maxine came around the front and waited by the car. I thanked the lady and left. When I got back to the car, I asked Maxine if she was sure this was the place.

"Mr. Stewart, I'm telling you when I was here last night that lady was not here. There were two men and a woman that looked like Maggie sitting in the kitchen."

"Well, I guess they moved her to some other place. Let's take a ride down to City Hall and check the deed."

When we got to City Hall, we went to the hall of records and checked the house we just came from. The house was registered to a Mr. and Mrs. Carson from 1959 to 1969. In 1969 when Mr. Carson died, Mrs. Carson put the house in her name, using her maiden name Ms. Simms. Things were coming together. I got Vera on the car phone and asked her to check out Mr. Simms. I told her I needed the information tonight. Although I think I already knew the outcome. Vera said to me that Mama Castellano wanted to see me in Mr. Todd's office at three o'clock today. I was sure it had something to do with the Black Hand gang in Hong Kong. At any rate, I told Maxine to take me back to Alex's place first in Chinatown.

By the time we got to Alex's apartment, it was noon. I told Maxine to wait in the car, and I went inside. When I got to Alex's apartment, he and his father-in-law were having a loud discussion. It was about him keeping the money he swindled from Hong Kong. I came in the middle of the debate and listened for the time being.

It seems Mr. Simms had contacted them by phone. He gave them twenty-four hours to turn his share of the money over to him. If not, his daughter would be killed and sent back to him in a bag.

"Mr. Chong, what is more important to you, your daughter, or the money?" I said.

"Mr. Stewart, without the money, I don't have a daughter."

I didn't quite understand what he meant by that and told him so. He went on to explain.

"Mr. Stewart, you or Mr. Lomax don't know my daughter. When she was much younger, she couldn't handle the poverty; we had in Vietnam. She told me she would get a job working as a translator on an American base in Saigon. That's what she did. Her one goal at that time was to meet an American and marry him so she could come to America. Along came Alex, she found him attractive, and she made herself fall in love with him. Only as a means for her to obtain entry to America."

"Are you saying Maggie only married me to get back to the States?"

"Exactly, Mr. Lomax."

"That's a bunch of bull shit Mr. Chong; Maggie wouldn't do that. I know Maggie, and she is not that type of person."

I could tell Alex was feeling hurt, and that meant trouble. I knew that whenever Alex got hurt, he would throw up this wall of anger to hide his hurt. His reasoning would become unbalanced. I tried to calm him down.

"Wait, Alex, let's hear it all. Go ahead, Mr. Chong, finish what you were saying."

"Thank you, Mr. Stewart. Anyway, after she married Alex, she came to me and said, well, pop, step one was accomplished. I don't think she meant to hurt you, Alex. Her marriage started as a convenience for her to get what she wanted. Later she fell in love with you. After that incident with that little girl, you hit with your car. She tried to keep things in the right perspective so you wouldn't go off the deep end. She tried to keep the marriage together. The more you drank and got out of hand, the more pressure it put on her. By the time you settled here in New York, she was walking on a fragile line of her own. Her feelings about the poverty that she remembered in Vietnam were stronger than her love for you. That's when your troubles began."

"What a minute, I don't have to listen to a meddling old man that doesn't know what the hell he's talking about."

"Alex, let's hear him out."

Alex turned away and walked to the window. It was hard for him to swallow all this at one time. I knew this, but he had to hear it.

"Continue, Mr. Chong."

"By the time I got to San Francisco, she was at her wit's end. She wrote to me and said she was going to leave Alex only I talked her out of it. For the time being anyway. Then later, when I wrote and told her to come to San Francisco, she called me long distance. She told me she had made up her mind. That's when she disappeared."

"Brent, are you going to believe all this fried rice he's spitting out about Maggie?"

"I don't know what to believe right now. I do know you both should be thinking about how you can get Maggie back, alive and in one piece. Then we can approach the other problem. I must see a very heavy-duty lady later today about the money you took from a certain organization in Hong Kong. What are you going to do about that?"

"I don't know, Mr. Stewart."

"Well, the way I see it, you don't have too many choices. If you promise to give back the money to your friends in Hong Kong, I might be able to work out a deal with them. They might be willing to let you have the money long enough to get Maggie back. Then they will deal with Mr. Simms and his associates. What do you think?"

"Sounds plausible but not logical, those people I did business with are not too forgiving with people that steal from them."

"I know that Mr. Chong, but let's cross one bridge at a time. I have this meeting to go to this afternoon. Let's wait and see what they say. Okay?"

"All right, I'll wait and see what they say."

"Well, both of you are crazy as a hoot owl, and I'm going to get back Maggie my way."

Alex started for the door, and I stepped in the way to stop him. He took a swing at me. He was much slower then he used to be. I moved aside and threw a right that landed on his jaw, and he went down. I guess I hit him a little harder than I wanted to. He was out like a light. I helped him to a chair. Maybe a couple of days in jail might cool him off. Besides then I wouldn't have to worry about him. I'd know where he was all the time.

Bill Singer owed me a favor. I called him, told him what happened, asked him to hold him for a couple of days on some trumped-up charges until I could figure something out. He was furious but agreed to it and said he was on his way over. I gave him the address and told him I would explain everything to him later and hung up.

I picked up Alex and put him on the couch. He was out like a light.

"Do you think he is all right?"

"Of course, Mr. Chong. He'll be a little sore when he comes to, not to mention a little mad at me. Other than that, he'll be just fine."

I figured this was as good a time as any to have a chat with Mr. Chong. So, I asked him whatever possessed him to take the diamonds?

"Mr. Stewart, when you have nothing in your life, and the opportunity arises for you to have something like those diamonds. You take it."

He had a point there, and I didn't have a reply.

"But you are going to give the diamonds; back, aren't you?"

"I guess I must. I love my daughter very much. I hope it isn't too late."

"Mr. Chong, I may have a solution to our problem. I'll let you know tonight."

Just then there was a knock at the door. When I asked who it was, I could recognize the voice of my old friend Bob Singer from police headquarters. I looked over at the couch as I opened the door. Alex was starting to come around.

Bob walked in with two-uniformed cops. Mr. Chong looked a little surprised. He thought he was going to be arrested.

Bob said, "Brent, are you sure you want to do this?"

"Yes, let's get on with it. I don't want Alex doing anything he'll be sorry for later. Just keep him for a couple of hours and give him a chance to think. He'll be okay."

The two uniformed cops helped Alex to his feet and lead him out the door while reading him his rights. Mr. Chong and I followed them outside, and I told Maxine to take Mr. Chong back to my mother's place in Brooklyn. I also told her to drop me off at Mr. Todd's office. Then pick me up after the meeting, on her way back from Brooklyn.

CHAPTER NINE

Maxine pulled up in front of the Castellanos building on Park Avenue, and I got out. I told Maxine to pick me up on her way back from Brooklyn and went inside. Susan was sitting at her desk, typing away. I said, hello.

"Ah, Mr. Stewart, won't you be seated, and I'll tell Mr. Todd you are here. They are expecting you."

She called Mr. Todd on the intercom and told him I was here. A few minutes later, Mr. Todd came out and greeted me and asked me to follow him in the office.

When I went inside his office, it was like an instant replay of the last time I was there. Mama was sitting on the couch between her two faithful companion sons. They reminded me of those two lion statues that sit on either side of the New York public library as you enter.

Mr. Todd spoke, "Well, Mr. Stewart, your forty-eight hours is up. Do you have any news for me?"

"Yes, I know where the item that belongs to the Hei-Shou-Tang is. I want to make a deal with you."

"You're in no position to make any deal."

Just then, Mama spoke, "Jack, let's hear him out first. Go ahead, Mr. Stewart, finish what you were saying."

"Thank you, Mrs. Castellano. Well, first, we would like to keep the items long enough to get Maggie back, secondly after we give back the items. I want your word that no harm will come to Mr. Chong or his daughter."

It was about this time that Sonny had his say in the matter.

He jumped up and said, "Bull-Shit."

Jack told him to sit and be quiet and then turned to me and spoke.

"And why should we do this for you, Mr. Stewart?"

"The only reason I could think of is that it would stop a lot of unnecessary bloodshed. Also, you don't need the bad publicity."

Jack looked at Mama, and Mama shook her head ever so lightly. Jack looked back at me and spoke once again.

"Okay, we'll do it, but we will have some of our people watching you. To look out for our interest, you understand."

I agreed and left. When I walked out of the office, Susan was smiling and flipped me the okay sign. I smiled back and walked out.

Well, all I have to do now find out where Maggie is. Then talk her father into giving me the diamonds. I'd say I have my hands full. It was too soon for Maxine to make it back from Brooklyn. I decided to get a bite to eat while I waited. I saw one of those guys on the corner; you know the ones that sell hot dogs. I went over and bought a soft drink and a hot dog with the works. My stomach would later make me regret it, but what the hell. One of the things I liked about eating from one of those stands is watching the people that walk by. I still think that some of the prettiest women in the world walk around New York City, also some of the strangest people. I looked at my watch and realized I had been in Mr. Todd's office for almost two hours. I decided to call Bob downtown and tell him to let Alex go. I felt guilty about leaving him as long as I did. So, I called Bob and told him to let Alex go home and then went ahead and started to finish my hot dog.

While I was eating, I noticed my two Asian buddies from San Francisco were standing outside the Castellano building. Mama said she would have somebody watching me. I didn't know it was going to be Hong Kong's answer to Laurel and Hardy or Starski and Hutch. I waved them to follow me as I walked down the street toward the Pam Am building and ate my hot dog.

Just then, I noticed a car following Laurel and Hardy. Mama wasn't taking any chances.

By the time I got a few blocks up to the entrance to Riverside drive, Maxine was pulling up. I climbed in and told her to head for the office. As we drove off, I could see my two friends jump in the car and follow. I picked up the phone and called in to see if there were any messages. Vera said that Alex called and said that he heard from Mr. Simms. I hung up and told Maxine to head over to Alex's apartment. He had plenty of time to cool down. Besides, I spent one night in the slammer a few years ago, and it seemed like an eternity. He wasn't going to be so happy about what I had done. But I'm sure I could make him understand. Maxine told me she dropped Mr. Chong off at Alex's place instead of Brooklyn she knew I would want him at Alex. Smart lady, when we got there, I told her to wait out front and to keep the engine running while I went in to see Alex.

When I got inside the restaurant, Alex was sitting at the bar with Mr. Chong and Suzy.

"Well, I see everybody is present. Okay, let's get down to business. What did you hear?"

At first, Alex didn't say anything. He walked up to me and looked at me. I could tell by the look on his face Alex was upset. Before I knew what had happened, he hit me with a right cross that sent me whirling to the floor.

"That's for looking out for me. I don't like jails. Thanks anyway. I might have done something crazy."

"Anything else you want to say before I get up?"

"Well, yes, Mr. Simms has gotten greedy. He wants us to bring him all the diamonds in a suitcase by Friday. That gives us two days to figure out a plan."

I got up and said, "Where does he want us to meet him?"

"Not us. You. Simms thinks I'm too close to the situation, and Mr. Simms doesn't trust Mr. Chong. Maggie told him about you. He wants you to bring it to the boardwalk down at Seaside Heights at noon, by the entrance to the rides."

"Well, I guess that's the long and the short of it. Mr. Chong, will you give me the diamonds to get your daughter back?"

"I don't have a choice in this matter. Yes, of course, I will."

I told Mr. Chong to give me the jacket, and I would arrange everything, then I left. As I headed back to the office, I formulated a plan to get Maggie back. I was going to need Maxine's help, and I told her so. She said yes. I knew that she would. Ever since I opened this office, Maxine said she was looking for some excitement. Well, it looked as though she was finally going to get what she wanted.

When I got back to the office, Vera told me she had some news. That little girl that Alex had run over in Saigon has been adopted by a prominent doctor in Los Angeles a Dr. John Austin. After she left the Military hospital in Saigon, she went back to the orphanage just outside Saigon and stayed there for a year. Dr. John Austin is a bone specialist. He was requested to make a trip to the orphanage in 1980. To care for some of the hard cases that are at the orphanage. He came across Kim and fell in love with her. He and his wife decided to adopt Kim. They brought her back to live in Los Angeles in '82. I told Vera to get their address in Los Angeles. In the meantime, I wanted to have a talk with Maxine about Friday. If I was going to get Maggie and the diamonds back, I was going to have to do some tall thinking.

The day turned out to be longer than I thought. When it was all over, I called Suzy to see if she wanted to go to dinner. She said she would meet me at the apartment at seven o'clock and asked me to let Millie go home early. I called Johnny at the garage and told him to let Suzy in upstairs. As I was looking over Friday's plan and hoping it would come off okay, Vera came in to say good-bye.

"Mr. Stewart, I'm going home for the day if you don't need me."

"That's fine, Vera. I'll see you tomorrow. Make yourself a note. I want to talk to Maxine tomorrow first thing."

"Right, Mr. Stewart, I'll do that right now. Bye."

I didn't realize how exhausted I was until I headed for the elevator. I pushed the button for the penthouse and waited. As the elevator doors opened, I saw this vision of loveliness standing there wearing my bathrobe and a drink in her hand.

"Here you go, Brent. A drink to relax you, dinner will be ready in a couple of minutes. Why don't you hop in the shower in the meantime."?

"Suzy, you sure know how to make a man feel good."

I put my arms around that soft body, caressed it like it was a life support system, right now it felt like one. Suzy was good for me. I went in, got undressed, and took my well-needed shower. When I got out, dinner was on the table.

"Hmmm smells good, what is it."

"It's my special recipe of Cantonese Chicken and Mushrooms. How do you like it?"

I tasted it, and it melted in my mouth. I didn't realize how hungry I was.

"It's delicious."

"I'm glad you like it."

After dinner was over, I told Suzy to leave the dishes for Millie. We went out on the patio to have a drink and to look at my city. It was one of those beautiful spring evenings. You could see a thousand stars in the sky. The moon was a quarter full; you could see some clouds float by, and the stars would disappear and reappear again. I took Suzy in my arms and kissed her. I love to run my fingers through her long black hair. It felt like silk, and her lips were like the soft outside of a peach.

"Brent, I want you to know that these last couple of weeks with you have been the best time of my life."

"You know Suzy, and I was just going to say the same thing."

We kissed again. I put my arms around Suzy, and we walked into the bedroom where the night promised to be like heaven. She laid down on the bed and looked up at me while she undid her robe. Her body looked beautiful with the night sky reflecting off it from the patio. I laid down next to her and caressed her body. She excited me like no other woman I have ever known. Her nipples got hard to my touch, and when I kissed each one, I thought they would burst. Our passions rose as the night faded, and our bodies did what bodies do best.

CHAPTER TEN

Thursday went by without anything unusual happening. I went over everything with Maxine that we were going to do on Friday. I told Alex and Mr. Chong to stay put, and I would get in touch with them later after the exchange. I contacted Bill Singer at the police station and told him everything I was going to do. He had no jurisdiction on the Jersey side, but he had some friends down at the Toms River Police. He contacted them and told them what was coming down. They said they would have a few plainclothesmen on the boardwalk to watch everything at the time of the exchange. All I had to do was to stop by the station house on my way to the beach. Talk to Mr. Snyder so he could see who the good guys were.

Maxine and I headed down to Toms River early. We took two cars in case anything came up. I left first in my RX7, and Maxine followed in a rented Chevy. I wanted to make sure that no one could follow. I had Maxine take a different route. Then double back on to the Southern State Parkway South and meet me at the Toms River Police Station.

When I arrived, I waited outside the police station for Maxine. She showed up about thirty minutes after I did. We went inside to talk to Mr. Snyder.

Mr. Snyder was just about what I expected. He was about five feet ten and overweight. Mr. Snyder had been on the force for twenty-five years and didn't have any plans of retiring until they forced him. He agreed to go along with me. Mr. Snyder said he would have men planted north and south of the rides on the boardwalk. Mr. Snyder wouldn't close in until the exchange unless he heard gunfire.

It was eleven when we headed over to the boardwalk. I told Maxine to stand by the Mouse ride. That way she had a good view of the Midway and me. I was standing by the Cotton candy stand. We waited. This time of the year, it didn't start to get very crowded until mid-afternoon. A few little kids were pulling their Mom and Dads around the boardwalk, rushing them from one side to the other. A cute elderly couple walked by. They looked like it was their first trip here, and they looked like they were enjoying it. It was then that I caught sight of Maggie walking down the boardwalk towards me. She was with a tall, blonde-haired gentleman. They walked up to me very carefully and told me to keep walking with them.

"Maggie, are you, all right?"

"Yes."

"Don't worry, just do everything I say, and things will be all right."

"No, Brent, you do what we say, and everything will be okay. Hand me the briefcase."

It looked like Mr. Chong was right about Maggie, shit. I asked her why.

"Why! Why! I'll tell you why, because I'm tired of penny-pinching and taking care of a drunk for ten years. That's why."

"Maggie, he loves you very much, and he needs you."

"Yeah, well, I needed him too to get to the states."

"Why this way, why didn't you just leave him when you got to the states?"

"I had nothing, and I knew nobody I had to stay with him until something better came along. Then Jack here called me from Hong Kong. We hadn't seen each other since Saigon when Jack was in the Army working at the Headquarters building. He told me about my father's plan, and I was going to run away with him and his share of the diamonds. When his partner got killed before Jack could leave Hong Kong, Jack called me again. Told me he had set up his partner. Now there were just the two of them. Jack had a plan on how to get all the diamonds. I said, okay."

"Maggie, there is still time to change your mind."

"You don't get it, do you, Brent. I don't want to change my mind. I want diamonds. I want nice things. I need nice things. Enough talking, give me the briefcase now."

"Maggie, you can't get away with this, the authorities know everything. They have this boardwalk covered."

Just then, Jack grabbed the briefcase and Maggie and backed away.

"Okay, smartass, we're getting out of here, and if anybody tries to stop us, she gets it in the back."

"Michael, it was you that killed Sammy because he was getting too close. It was also you that hit me on the head when I surprised you at Lilies flat."

"You have all the answers, don't you, Mr. P.I."?

Maggie looked at Jack in shock.

"Sorry sweetheart, I'll only needed you for a little while longer."

"Jack, you said you loved me. We were going to go away together."

"Maggie, He used you just like he used his partner. He was after the diamonds all the time. He never loved you. He needed you just like you needed Alex."

"No, no, it isn't true. It isn't true. Tell Brent; Jack, tell him it isn't true."

"It is the truth, baby. I needed you and your slant-eyed father. When he came to me with the idea in Hong Kong, I jumped at it. Come on, let's get out of here."

Just then, Maggie pushed Jack away and grabbed for the diamonds. The gun went off and hit Maggie in the back she fell. Jack took off with the crystals. Two of the plainclothes cops came running up and shouted.

"Stop, we're Police."

They fired two warning shots in the air. Jack turned and fired one shot hitting one of the officers. The other officer fired two shots. One hit the briefcase shattering it and spilling the diamonds on the boardwalk they all scattered and fell between the cracks into the ocean. The second gunshot fired by the officer hit Jack in the chest. Jack went down. I rushed to Maggie; she was lying on the boardwalk. Maxine was comforting her; the bullet had entered the back. She looked up at me.

"Brent, I'm sorry things didn't work out the way you wanted them too. Tell Alex I'm sorry for hurting him. I...I... lov...."

She was gone. I didn't know what I was going to tell Alex. All I know is he wasn't going to find out the truth from me. I couldn't break his heart after all that has happened. Detective Snyder came over and said the ambulance was on his way.

"How is Mr. Simms?"

"I'm afraid he won't be, needing the diamonds where he's going, he bought it."

Well, this case was finished. Mr. Chong was deported back to Hong Kong. Neither government had a case against him. I'm sure the Hei Shou Tang will be looking for him. As for Mama Castellano, well, she was glad not to get her name or picture in the paper again. Alex was taking it hard. One good thing came out of all this. Kim Ho's father had operated on her four years ago, and she was now walking fine. Alex was going out to Los Angeles to visit her. Who knows, maybe Alex will be happy again? I hope so. As for me well, I guess I'll look for another case. Life goes on. Suzy, well, she got the best deal of all. She got me.

www.ingramcontent.com/pod-product-compliance
Lightning Source LLC
Chambersburg PA
CBHW021736010826
48973CB00016B/616